Petteril's

Lord Petteril Mysteries, Book 2

Mary Lancaster

Petteril's Corpse

Chapter One

L ord Petteril gazed up at the sky, calculating how long it would take for the rain to arrive. His horses, beautifully matched greys, shifted restlessly, shaking their heads, bored at standing still so long and, no doubt, looking forward to their next meal. Petteril, who still thought of himself by his Christian name of Piers, knew how they felt.

He sniffed the air, as though he might smell rain approaching, but all he caught was the earthy scent of forests and, somewhere in the distance, a hint of burning wood.

He sighed. "You had better come out," he called to a large rhododendron bush close to the path, nestling between two young elm trees. "Or we'll all get soaked."

The bush moved, leaves fluttering and causing Piers to hope, but otherwise nothing happened.

"Do you need help?" he enquired.

"No," said the bush defiantly.

"Then hurry up. I don't choose to arrive at my ancestral acres in the guise of drowned rat with semi-drowned servant."

Nothing happened. The bush remained still and silent. He could almost imagine it was glaring at him.

Piers sighed. "Ape," he said warningly.

The bush moved and a grumpy figure in a blue calico dress squeezed out between it and the elm tree. Under one arm she clutched a bundle of grey-ish clothing. Her other hand held a scrap of white linen. The dress fitted her shape and height perfectly, though clearly

1

not her mood. She scowled through her tangle of short, golden-fair hair and marched across to the curricle.

Controlling the twitch of his lips, Piers leaned over and stretched down one hand to help her up. She jerked out of his reach, snapping, "I can manage, for Gawd's sake, I been jumping up and hanging onto the back of this thing for weeks."

"Then get on with it," Piers commanded. "Or you'll have to jump up on the back again."

"I'd rather," she muttered, clambering onto the seat beside him with no grace whatsoever, and roundly cursing her skirts. With unnecessary force, she shoved the roll of clothes into the carpet bag at her feet.

Piers handed her a comb from his pocket and took the white, linen cap from her clutching fingers. Ungraciously, she dragged the comb through her locks, and he plonked the cap on her head. She tossed the comb onto the seat between them and with quick, deft fingers, tied the strings beneath her chin.

"I look ridiculous," she muttered.

She didn't. She looked like a sullen, respectable, awkwardly pretty girl of some indeterminate lower class, in an old fashioned dress. Her age could have been anything between sixteen and twenty summers. Ape was April once more,

"You'll do," Piers replied. "If you stop sulking and can avoid challenging the boot boy to a wrestling match."

"Who's the boot boy?" she asked suspiciously.

"I have no idea."

"I could be the boot boy," she said with such regret that he nudged her.

"No, you couldn't. You're a girl."

The trouble was, she had taken on the guise of a boy so long ago that she didn't even think of herself as female anymore. Her skirts irked her, and she walked and talked like Ape, the street urchin she'd been when Piers first encountered her burgling his house some four weeks ago. For reasons that still were not clear to him, he had employed the child in his own stable until he had realized how unsuitable the arrangement was for one neither child nor boy. The only way he had got her to agree to living as a girl again was to promise her she could make the change between London and his country seat of Haybury. Even so, she had stretched it out until the last moment. They were a bare five miles from his house, Haybury Court.

She sniffed. "I won't fit in."

That was probably true. Mrs. Park, his London housekeeper, had managed to civilize her to some degree, but Ape/April still tended to swear like a sailor and do what she wanted rather than what she was told.

"It will be an adjustment," he allowed. The thread of an idea was working through his mind, but he would have to meet the staff first and, more to the point, consult Ape—April—once she had stopped sulking.

He flicked the reins, and the horses moved on.

"Can you smell burning?" April asked suddenly.

"Someone burning garden waste. The village is just beyond the wood."

She shook her head, not with impatience but unease that was almost dread. "No, there's more n' wood. It's like...plague."

"Plague!" He blinked at her. "What on earth do you mean?"

"Maybe not plague but, you know, sickness. When people get ill, and everyone catches it and loads of 'em die and they have to burn their clothes in—" She broke off, her eyes widening. "That's it. It's burning clothes. Who'd burn clothes if they didn't have plague?"

It made an uneasy kind of sense. April had grown-up in the crowded slums of the east end docks and St. Giles, where bouts of illness were devastating to people already poor, exhausted and malnourished.

Piers sniffed the air again and turned his head into the wind. "It's not in the village either. It's too close."

He pulled up the horses once more and from habit, April jumped down to go to the horses' heads while he alighted. However, without a word, Piers looped the reins around a tree and strode off toward the smoky smell, April at his heels.

"There." She pointed past him to a small clearing, where smoke issued in a lethargic kind of way from an indeterminate heap.

They walked toward it. There was no fire left, only a pile of ash and a few singed, smoking rags. Piers, glancing around the clearing, saw another, much worrying sight only a few feet away. He swerved toward it.

A man, naked as the day he was born, lay face down on the gravelly ground. Quickly, Piers crouched beside him, reaching for his wrist and searching for a pulse, but he already knew he wouldn't find one. The flesh was chillingly cold and stiff and had been dead for some time.

Piers released the rigid wrist and sat back on his heels. The dead man had a full head of dark brown hair, cut fashionably short. What Piers could see of his face looked to be about Piers's his own age, six-and-twenty, and the body looked trim and fit. Death had taken him tragically young, which was upsetting in itself. What bothered Piers more was the dried blood staining the ground around him.

April swore.

Hastily, Piers rose and began to unbutton his coat.

"Don't use your coat," April commanded, already running back the way they had come. "I'll bring a blanket."

While she was gone, Piers heaved the man over far enough to see the knife buried to the hilt in his chest. He let the man fall back as April's returning footsteps thudded through the undergrowth. Tripping over her skirts, she all but threw the horse blanket over the corpse.

"That's blood on the ground, isn't it?" she said in a detached sort of way.

"I think so, yes."

"He wouldn't burn his clothes before killing hisself, would he? And laying hisself out so undignified."

"Unlikely," Piers agreed. He drew the blanket a few inches farther up to cover the dead man's head, then turned and walked back to the remains of the fire, which he poked with his toe.

"Can't have been an accident, neither," April remarked.

"No."

"Someone croaked him. Look at the way his hand's reaching, as if he were trying to crawl. He didn't just stab hisself and lie down to die."

He could have changed his mind when it was too late. A tragedy that paralyzed Piers because he understood it only too well. *There, but for the grace of...* Unexpectedly, April took his hand, tugging him away. Her grip was surprisingly gentle, as if she knew the bleak, black memories conjured into his brain. She probably did.

"You can't do nothing for him," she said briskly, letting him go as soon as he began to stride toward the horses and the curricle. "'Cept find out who he is."

"And who—er... croaked him," Piers said. "I wonder who the magistrate is around here?"

"Might be you." Her smile was crooked. "Wouldn't that be something?"

APRIL—SHE SUPPOSED, reluctantly, that the name had more dignity than Ape which had served well enough for the back streets of St. Giles—was concerned for his lordship. Throughout her life, she had seen death in many forms, including by violence. It wasn't that she didn't care the poor cove was dead. She just cared more that Lord Petteril wouldn't think it was suicide.

Which it could have been. Despite what she'd said to him, she suspected a disturbed and desperate person might just decide to leave the world as they came into it. He could have fallen on the knife whose hilt she had seen sticking out of his chest. And he was a nob. April could tell by the cut of his hair and the smoothness of his hands. And young, surely still in his twenties. These similarities to Petteril were not lost on her and she didn't want his lordship reverting to old ideas or states of mind.·

So, forgetting about her annoying skirts, she passed the rest of the journey speculating who the dead man was and why anyone would have burned his clothes.

"Waste," she commented. "Good money in decent clothes."

"Not worth it if you're caught selling a dead man's rig," Lord Petteril pointed out.

"Suppose," she said doubtfully. "Why d'you think he burned 'em, then?"

"Anger, hatred. Or to make it harder to identify the victim."

"Can't be hard in a place like this. There's no other people."

To April, this was the most surprising thing of all about the countryside they had passed through since leaving London. Vast swathes of fields and forests, hedges, meadows, with no buildings, no people, only animals. Much of it was very pretty, but in truth it made her uneasy.

They beat the oncoming rain to the viscount's house, Haybury Court, but only just. April barely noticed the weather for her sheer awe at the size of the dwelling which came suddenly into view as the horses swept up a somewhat neglected driveway marred by creeping weeds and uneven stones.

"Cor," April breathed. It made Lord Petteril's London residence look like a cottage. A massive stone building like a castle at the top, but with huge number of elegant windows that gleamed, even in the grey gloom. It had pillars and carvings in the stone and extended even around the corner she could see. A ruin of some other building, with foliage growing out of it, could be seen in the grounds, surrounded by gardens and bright, colourful spring flowers. "It's a bloody palace. Did you live there?"

"No. Spent quite a lot of time here as a boy, though. A few Christ-mases, most summers. Haven't been back for a long time. Six or seven years."

His handsome face was veiled, hiding whatever he felt about the place. He had inherited it and the title after the deaths of his father, brother, uncle and two cousins. The family had bad luck by anyone's standards.

"Do they know you're coming?" April asked, a shade nervously.

"Well, I certainly wrote to the housekeeper and told her so." He glanced at her. "You'll come in the front door with me, and I'll speak to Mrs. Hicks about you."

"I'd rather work in the stables," April said. "I never cleaned any-thing else in my life."

"Nonsense. I saw you wash your face only yesterday."

She stuck her tongue out at him and was gratified to see the twinkle of an incipient smile in his eyes.

"You don't stick out your tongue out at Lord Petteril," he said gravely.

"And I don't call you mister, and I don't swear, and I don't wear boy's clothes." She sighed and he nudged her with one arm before bringing the horses to a snorting halt by the front door.

"It's an adventure," he said, and she had to swallow her scornful re-ply as a buxom woman sailed down the front steps at the same time as a couple of grooms loped round from the far side of the house.

"My lord, welcome!" beamed the woman, presumably the house-keeper.

"Mrs. Hicks. A pleasure to see you again."

April quickly grabbed her bag and scrambled out of the curricle be-fore he did something daft like lift her down—which he'd done once on the journey while his mind was clearly somewhere else. When he'd noticed, she wasn't sure which of them had been more embarrassed.

A manservant also emerged to take the bags.

"Most of my baggage will follow with my valet and groom," Lord Petteril said, seeing Mrs. Hicks's surprise. "They should be here by mid-day."

The two grooms—an older man, all weather-beaten and lined with a game leg, and a young lad, tugged their caps at his lordship, dividing their awed attention between him and the grey horses.

April sneaked a quick pet on the near horse's neck before the grooms led them off.

"Come in out of the rain, my lord," Mrs. Hicks urged. She cast a curious, unfriendly look at April, especially when she trotted after them up the curved steps and through the impressive, tiled portico, and huge front door.

Inside was even more amazing, a huge hall with two fireplaces, bigger even than the drawing room of the London house which April had once peeked inside. A grand staircase led upward and, speechless, April climbed after Lord Petteril and the housekeeper.

"Tell, me, Mrs. Hicks," his lordship said, "who is the local magistrate these days?"

"Still Mr. Lindon, sir, though there's no denying Mr. Alleyn would like the honour. Now, Mr. Piers, I mean, my lord, they're bringing tea to the morning room, so just go in..."

"Come with me, Mrs. H.," he urged. "I need to send a quick note to Mr. Lindon. And we need to talk about staff."

She opened wide, scandalized eyes. "Before you've had refreshment, my lord?"

His lip twitched. "Indeed."

He obviously remembered the place well enough, for he paused outside a particular door and bowed Mrs. Hicks inside. April glared at him and his eyes gleamed as he turned and preceded her into the morning room—another huge apartment with large windows giving a fine view of the grey sky and the gardens.

Lord Petteril went straight to the elegant desk beneath one window and without sitting, pulled paper, ink and pen towards him. He inspected the pen's nib and appeared satisfied.

"Have you adequate staff, Mrs. Hicks?" he asked and, bending his long person, he commenced writing with a speed that left April slack-jawed. She could write her name now, and all the letters of the alphabet but she could never imagine making the words flow across the page as quick as thought.

"I took on another couple of girls from the village who're giving satisfaction," Mrs. Hicks pronounced. "So, I've plenty to keep the house as it should be and look after your lordship. Where we're short is male staff. Old Mr. Clarke—the butler, if you recall—retired years ago and with his lordship coming down so seldom, he was never replaced. Got Harry to do the heavy work, but I suppose you might want a couple of footmen as well as a butler if you're staying. Gardens and grounds could use some work as I'm sure you saw, but there's only old Ribble and his boy and it's too much for them."

"Indeed, I shall speak to Ribble," Lord Petteril said, still writing. It fascinated April that he could converse and apparently understand at the same time. "But you have enough female staff?"

"Quite." She cast a hostile, triumphant glance at April.

But April rejoiced. Maybe she could work in the stables after all. Or even the gardens though she didn't know the first thing about plants and flowers.

"You planning on staying, my lord?" Mrs. Hicks asked.

"For some time, at least," he replied, finishing his letter with a flourish and replacing the pen in the stand. "This is April," he said, waving one hand toward her. "I am training her to be my assistant."

Mrs. Hicks stared at him. So did April. He appeared oblivious, shaking sand from an elegant little pot over his paper and then blowing it off.

"Assistant in what?" Mrs. Hicks demanded.

"Whatever is required. A secretary at this moment. I still have my university interests, after all... She will require accommodation. The room on the top landing seems suitable.

"What, Nurse's old room?"

"Unless Nurse is still in it."

"Nurse died years ago, as you know very well, Mr. Piers!"

"Then I imagine it is free. Have it made up for April, if you would be so good." He folded the letter. "And send someone over to Lindon Grange with this as quickly as possible. It is important. And here is tea. Wonderful."

Mrs. Hicks took the letter like one in a trance, then she blinked and walked past the maids ferrying in trays of tea and scones and sandwiches.

April stood awkwardly, still in the cloak Petteril had given her, while he sprawled in an armchair and politely thanked the maids who were secretly if avidly observing him. April waited until they had gone, leaving the door open, before marching up to him.

"Secretary! I can't even *read*!"

"Yes, you can. You can even write."

"Not like you! What are you up to? She hates me, now!"

He glanced at her. "You're not pretending you care?"

She flushed. "I got to eat with her. And the other servants."

"Yes, you better had or they'll gossip all the more. I have every faith in you to get round them, like you did Mrs. Park and the others."

"What do you really want me to do?" she demanded.

His lips curved. "Assist me in learning about our corpse."

Chapter Two

Mr. Lindon, known locally as the Squire, was announced in the middle of the afternoon.

By then, Piers had briefly inspected the house, including the rooms that had once been his uncle's and were now by tradition his. They were pleasant enough apartments, and they had been aired, cleaned and warmed, but, somehow, they still *smelled* of the late viscount. Piers opened all the windows and was actually glad when Stewart, his valet, arrived with his things, including a trunk full of books and another of clothes. Piers had hopes that by evening the place would feel more familiar.

"Do you want these books placed in the library, my lord?" Stewart asked. "Or on the shelves here?"

"Here," Piers replied firmly. Deciding to leave his valet to it, he strolled to the door and paused. "I hope you'll be comfortable enough in Haybury Court."

"I'm sure I will be. Seems a pleasant place, and I like the country."

He nodded. "I don't wish to burden you with excessive responsibilities, but I have taken on an assistant. Her name is April."

If Stewart's hands paused in removing the books from the trunk, it was so infinitesimal Piers might have imagined it. "I'll look out for her, my lord."

"Thank you." Piers was only too aware of the conjecture he might be causing, but there was really no simple way to do this. Stewart would almost certainly recognize April as Ape, but this was the best protection he could give her.

He went off to explore the library, which is where he still was when Mr. Lindon was announced.

"Oh, show him in," Piers told the maid, leaping off the third step of the wheeled ladder attached to the bookshelves.

The maid might have giggled on her way out, but a few moments later, she came back with his guest, curtseying with perfect propriety.

Piers had met Lindon before, as a boy, and certainly there was something familiar about the man's face, as he walked into the library. In distinguished middle age, he was greying at the temples and inclined to stoutness. He dressed like a country gentleman, his clothes expensive, but comfortable without any of the excesses of fashion, and despite the signs of worry in his face, he smiled at Piers with apparent pleasure.

"My lord, very happy indeed to see you at Haybury Court!"

"Thank you," Piers replied, offering his hand and looking for some distinctive feature by which he could recognize the squire in the future. Faces were a problem for him. "It's a pleasure to be back, although mixed as you might imagine."

Lindon wrung Piers's hand with both of his, nodding sagely. "Of course, of course. So many tragedies in one family. Most sad. Most difficult for you. You have all our condolences, though we are glad to have you here as viscount."

Assuming Lindon had not adopted the royal "we", Piers gathered he spoke for the neighbourhood. Whether or not the neighbourhood agreed.

"Glass of wine?" Piers offered. "I found a very fine old sherry my uncle must have horded."

"Don't mind if I do," Lindon said, rubbing his hands together and taking the chair by the fire which Piers indicated.

Piers poured two glasses of sherry from the tray he'd already had brought in before luncheon.

"Bit of a nasty surprise," Lindon commented, accepting his glass with a nod of thanks, "discovering a corpse on your homecoming."

"Wouldn't have known anything about it if my assistant hadn't smelled the burning."

Lindon shook his head sadly and sipped his sherry. "Bad business. Poor fellow. I gather it was you who covered him? I left the blanket with Mrs. Hicks."

"Who is he?" Piers asked.

"The corpse? A stranger, apparently. The constables had never seen him before. Probably a vagrant. A lot of them are a bit...eccentric, though I've never known one burn his own clothes before."

Piers frowned. "Oh, I don't think he's a vagrant. His hands are too clean, his hair too well cut."

Lindon's eyebrows rose. "Do you say so? Maybe I should take a look. The constables reckoned he had stabbed himself."

"On what grounds?" Piers asked politely.

Lindon began to look slightly harassed. "On the grounds he fell on his knife," he said tartly. "And on the grounds no one around here would have murdered a total stranger."

"The question is, what was a total stranger—a genteel total stranger by the look of him—doing in my woods in the middle of the night."

Lindon pursed his lips in a sententious kind of way. "Well, we don't know how long he lay there."

"We can guess," Piers said gently. "Rigor mortis had set in, so he died at least six hours before I discovered him, and no more than twenty four. Judging by how long the fire might smoulder—assuming it was started at around the same time he died—my best guess would be that death occurred around two or three in the morning. Perhaps four at a pinch."

Lindon closed his slack mouth with a snap. "You think so?"

Piers swallowed some sherry. "Guessing," he admitted. "Knew some students of medicine at Oxford. I'll come with you to look at the body, if you like. Where is it?"

"In the Red Lion cellar," Lindon said without enthusiasm. "Dr. Rose is going to examine him. For the coroner, you understand."

Piers regarded him. "Aren't you the least curious? If he's not a vagrant—which I'd be willing to wager a fortune on—it's possible you might even know him."

"The constables know everyone," Lindon said testily. "And if they don't, Dr. Rose does. I actually came here to ask if *you* knew the deceased."

Piers, relieved to see some intelligence behind the man's indifference, took another sip of sherry. "No, I didn't, but then I didn't see him very clearly." And it would have made very little difference if he had. He *hoped* he didn't know the man. "Wouldn't mind another look, and we'll take my assistant who notices more than I do." At least in terms of faces. He set down his glass. "Did you come in your coach?"

Lindon finished his sherry and gave in to the inevitable. When summoned, April appeared, looking unusually neat and demure, still with her linen cap over her hair, and clutching the notebook Piers had given her and his other literacy students in London. Lindon blinked at her in some surprise, and when they reached his coach waiting at the front of the house, he seemed unsure whether he should hand her in.

Piers, knowing her dislike of physical contact, ushered the squire into his own coach first, and leapt up after him, leaving April to climb up herself and sit with her back to the horses. Piers saw her grinning to herself—she wasn't used to such luxury—and hoped she wouldn't say *Cor*.

The Red Lion was located in the heart of Haybury village. Barnes, the innkeeper knew enough to bow to Piers and mutter, "Welcome home, m'lord," took them into the cellar.

"Recognize him, Barnes?" Lindon asked as they clattered down the steps.

"No, sir. He never stayed at the Lion whether to eat, drink, or sleep."

Lindon sighed.

The corpse was laid out on a sheet on a large bench, surrounded by barrels, bottles and boxes. Candles had been lit to supplement the meagre light coming in through the short, narrow windows almost at ceiling height. A vaguely familiar figure was bent over the body, though he straightened as the others entered, and even drew another sheet up to decently cover the dead man.

"Ah, Rose, I brought Lord Petteril, who discovered the body," Lindon said.

"My lord. Welcome home."

"Thank you, Doctor." Piers offered his hand, since he could discern no sign of gore on the doctor's. "Good to see you again. What do you think of our poor friend here?"

Dr. Rose shrugged. "Male, in his twenties and in apparently excellent health. Of good circumstances, judging by his personal habits."

"A merchant, perhaps?" Lindon asked, sounding unaccountably hopeful.

"Possibly. Hard to tell with only the burnt rags of his clothing."

At least the doctor—or someone—had collected those. The few scraps of material and buttons sat in a tray on top of barrel. With a flick of his eyes, Piers directed April to it and she moved discreetly closer. He had often found it interesting how no one observed servants, particularly maidservants.

"How did he die, Doctor?" Piers asked. "Could it have been suicide?"

Rose pulled down the cover again to reveal the bruised, ragged wound in the man's chest. "It's possible," he said doubtfully. "Though the angle of the wound seems to have come from above, rather than straight as you might expect if he had done it himself."

"If someone else did it, wouldn't he have fallen on his back?" Lindon offered.

"Not necessarily. The knife is very sharp, and went straight into his heart. Death would have been pretty much instantaneous. I wouldn't rule suicide out just yet, but it looks to me as if someone murdered him."

Lindon groaned. "I'll send the constables to find out about strangers in the area. Both our friend, here, and anyone who might have..." He broke off awkwardly.

"Croaked him," Piers finished for him, without thinking. By the barrel-table, a small snort came from April, which fortunately no one seemed to notice. Both the doctor and Lindon were blinking at Piers in surprise. He pretended not to notice.

"Aren't you expecting a visitor, Lindon?" Rose said after a moment, turning toward the squire. "I'm sure Mrs. Lindon mentioned it to my wife."

"Hunter? Oh yes, but we don't expect him until tomorrow, and what the devil would he be doing in Petteril Wood in the middle of last night? It *was* last night this poor fellow died?"

Rose's eyebrows flew up. "I would think so. It could have been a few hours earlier but I would doubt it."

"What about the weapon that killed him?" Piers wondered, as the doctor pulled the sheet back over the corpse. "It looked like a hunting knife to me."

"It is," Rose replied, jerking his head toward another barrel table beside him. "Common looking thing, though."

Piers was forced to agree. He doubted they would discover either the killer or the identity of the victim through the weapon. He glanced at April.

"Couple of silver buttons," she said. "Scraps of clothing seem decent, but no maker's mark left on 'em."

Piers nodded approval of her observation, glad she had grasped what he wanted of her. Rose and Lindon stared at her in surprise, as if they had forgotten she was there. In the doctor's case, he might not even have noticed her before.

"Think he was fleeced, mi—my lord?" April, having almost addressed him as mister, sounded as if she had a mild stammer.

"You mean robbed?" Piers said thoughtfully.

"Well, the constables found no purse on him and a traveller of any degree would need money," Dr. Rose said. "He had no watch, either, nor rings nor anything else of value."

"Apart from two silver buttons," Piers said distractedly, observing them through one of his two quizzing glasses."

"Didn't old Alleyn get held up last week?" Lindon said, brightening suddenly at such a simple solution.

"Believe he did," Rose agreed. "Probably the fellow known locally as Brandy Bill, ever since he shared a toast with one of his victims down near Salisbury. Alleyn reckons he winged him. Over by Trowbridge on market day."

April reached a hand to her head as though she would scratch it, then hastily changed her mind as she encountered the linen of her cap. "Yes, but no gent of the high toby would burn decent clothes. Get good money for 'em or wear 'em hisself."

Mr. Lindon blinked several times. It was unclear whether he meant to rebuke her for talking to her betters uninvited or pour scorn on her statement.

"Fair point," Piers said. "No self-respecting thief would burn anything he could profit from. Even if he couldn't risk selling them locally, a highwayman moves around and could offload them anywhere. Seems to me the burning of the clothes was either an act of hatred or a feeble attempt to hide the status of his victim here."

"Not so feeble," Dr. Rose remarked. "We've no idea who he is."

Lindon sighed. "I'll send around to the other inns with a description of our man."

"Might enquire of the locals, too," Piers said mildly. "See if anyone was expecting a visitor."

Lindon began to look harassed. It was clear his magisterial duties up until now had been considerably less complicated. No doubt, he dealt more usually with domestic and property disputes, a few fights, perhaps the odd drunk behaving badly.

He glanced at his fob watch. "I'll look into it. But right now, I have to meet my wife and daughter." He straightened. "Perhaps your lordship would care to renew your acquaintance with them?"

"I should be delighted," Piers replied.

Leaving Dr. Rose to finish his examination, the others trooped up the cellar steps into the courtyard. The rain had gone off, but dampness still hung in the air. Two ladies were picking their way between the puddles, holding their skirts out of the dirt as far as was decorous, toward the waiting Lindon carriage.

The ladies caught sight of them emerging from the cellar and immediately veered toward them. For a moment, Piers was baffled to see two young women and wondered wildly if Lindon had been widowed and remarried to a much younger lady. Faces tended to blur in his memory at the best of times, but in these two women, he could recognize nothing.

They, however, recognized him. The lady in green smiled, her hand held out with obvious pleasure as she approached him. Close to, he saw the fine lines around her eyes, the softer definition of her jaw, but she was still a remarkably handsome woman, with no grey in her hair and no obvious thickening of her slender body.

"Lord Petteril!" she exclaimed. "What a pleasure to welcome you home at last, even in such sad circumstances."

She meant, of course, the death of his uncle, the previous viscount. And of his two male cousins and his own older brother, which had dumped the title squarely on his unwilling shoulders.

"How do you do, Mrs. Lindon?" he replied, taking her hand and bowing over it while her eyes raked him with interest. There was no grey visible in her dark hair, and her eyes were bright blue, though with an edge of hardness he had never noticed in his youth. "I am very glad to be back." It wasn't untrue, not yet at least.

"You remember Laura, of course." Mrs. Lindon smiled benignly. There was the tiniest hint of condescension in her manner, as though she were too used to being the lady of rank in any company. "Your childhood playmate."

Piers turned to the other woman, in palest pastel blue as suited a very young lady. His recollections of Laura Lindon were few, for she was several years younger than he. He remembered her brother Oscar more, though he would have been hard-pushed to conjure up his face.

The girl, smiling shyly at him was only about eighteen or nineteen summers, bright-eyed and pretty with shining dark hair of the same shade as her mother's, and the same fashionably willowy figure.

"Of course you won't remember me, my lord. I think I was only about ten years old when you were last here!"

Piers bowed over her hand, too. "I recall, but I confess I would not have known you."

It seemed a safe thing to say and before he had to converse further, Mrs. Lindon asked her husband, "Who was the man who fell in Petteril Wood? Is he ill or injured?"

Lindon shifted uncomfortably. "I'm afraid he is dead, my dear. And we have no idea who he is. He appears to be a passing traveller."

"Oh dear." Mrs. London's eyebrows suddenly flew up in alarm. "Oh dear! You don't suppose...surely, it could not be Lord Maxwell?"

"No, no, my dear," Lindon soothed. "What would Lord Maxwell Hunter be doing in his lordship's wood—on foot! —in the middle of the night? Besides, we don't expect him until tomorrow, do we?"

"No, that is true," Mrs. Lindon said distractedly, though she did not look entirely convinced. A cloud of worry crossed her fine eyes and she seemed to overcome it with an effort. "May we drop you off at the hall, my lord?"

"Ah, thank you, no," Piers said. "I believe I shall wander about the village for a bit to remind myself."

"Then you must come to tea. In fact, come tomorrow! We expect Lord Maxwell Hunter by then—I suppose you are acquainted?"

"I don't believe so." Piers was not acquainted with many aristocrats.

"Then we shall introduce you," Mrs. Lindon declared.

"Most kind." Petteril bowed again and stepped back to allow Lindon to hand his ladies into the carriage, then clapped his hat on his head and stood back for the carriage to make its way out of the yard.

Chapter Three

April quite enjoyed the walk back to the big house. The village seemed pretty, just a row or two of cottages, most of them small but still spacious by St. Giles standards, especially since in some only one or two people lived there. There was a square with a little church at one end, and a blacksmith's shop at the other. The Red Lion inn formed a third side and a patch of greenery the fourth, where a couple of children were playing.

"It's very quiet," April said dubiously. "Ain't you got any street sellers, costermongers and the like?"

"There's a general shop along the road, but mostly, the villagers eat what they grow, or what they can buy at the market in the next town. What do you think?"

"About this place or the dead cove?"

"Both, I suppose."

April shrugged to hide her pleasure to be asked about either. "It's not bad. And I think the dead cove was up to no good. Otherwise, like even the beak said, what was he doing in your wood in the dark? And where was his horse or whatever he came in? Nobs don't walk if they don't have to."

"My thoughts, more or less. Though please refrain from referring to Mr. Lindon—or any other justice of the peace—as the beak."

She sniffed. "Justice of the peace," she repeated scornfully. "He sounds like he never even seen a murdered cove before."

"He probably hasn't," Lord Petteril said mildly. "Neither have I."

She stared at him, stunned. "Really?"

"Really."

She couldn't quite read the expression in his eyes, but she supposed people in his world didn't get murdered much, if they stayed away from trouble. "What do you suppose he did?" she wondered aloud. "Our dead cove?"

"Maybe a little amateur poaching," Petteril mused. "Only he got caught by a nastier set of poachers from Trowbridge or somewhere further afield, who were annoyed to find him muscling in? Poaching is the most common crime around here. Nearly everyone turns a blind eye to it, though they don't care for the non-local variety."

"No sign of dead animals," April said. "Though I suppose the murdering poachers could have taken our man's as well as their own. And his weapon. Here, perhaps he was stabbed with his own hunting knife."

Lord Petteril grimaced.

"Or maybe the dead cove is the beak's visitor, done in by the high toby gent."

"Or someone else entirely. How many thieves do you know who would hang around to burn the evidence?"

"And risk bringing witnesses down on hisself," April added. "Though there's no houses near where we found him, is there? Maybe one of the nobs did him in for their own reasons."

"Such as?"

"How do I know why nobs do anything? But he's one of 'em, ain't he?"

"Probably. Did you notice there were no boots?"

"Or any footwear. Smoke would have smelled different. You reckon whoever killed him took his boots? 'Cause they're harder to get rid of?"

"It's a thought."

They walked on in silence, Petteril leading her along a path through fields and over a stream.

"It don't stink," she said suddenly. "London stinks in the rain. Here, it smells all...fresh and clean. The air don't stink. That's what's different."

She paused and twirled around, inhaling the sweet air, while gazing up at the sky. And when she came to a halt, he was watching her with an expression of indulgence, and something else she couldn't name.

"What?" she asked suspiciously, beginning to stride along again.

"You walk like a boy, but twirl like a girl."

She glared at him but could think of nothing to say.

"Give it a try," he coaxed.

"Give what a try?" she asked aggressively.

"Being a girl," he said.

She looked down, tore some leaves off a passing hedge, then glanced up again. "And if I can't be? If I hate it, I can be a boy again?"

He was silent, then, "If you want to be, I can't stop you."

He strode on faster, and she thought he was angry, but when she caught up with him, he didn't seem to be, just thoughtful, like he had been over the stolen necklace in London. She could understand that.

She didn't like that the dead cove had been killed on Lord Petteril's land. Not that she felt any grief, as such—how could she, when she didn't know him from Adam? —though she thought it disrespectful to strip the man naked only to burn his clothes. It wasn't the most horrific death she had seen, though it was an intriguing idea that one of the nobs might have done it themselves.

It was a puzzle, like the necklace had been a puzzle, and she was guiltily glad of the distraction.

BACK AT THE HOUSE, she let his lordship go in by the front door to his books or accounts or whatever he was doing and turned her reluctant steps to the stables. She had never been reluctant to see horses before, and in truth it wasn't the animals that had her dragging her heels, it was the humans.

By rights, she should be in the stables, looking after the viscount's horses. That was what he had hired her for in the first place. But girls couldn't be grooms or stable boys. Seemed to her girls couldn't do anything at all. Except wear ridiculous garments and not trip over them, which April was finding challenge enough.

A couple of grooms were gossiping in the stable yard. An old man and a very young one. They stopped long enough to gawp at her. Their eyes were insolently assessing, but since they had no idea who she was, they stopped short of insult. April ignored them, sailing inside in much the style of Lord Petteril's aunt.

The Professor whinnied at once, deserting his oats to straighten his head and peer over his stall door. April stroked his long nose and neck. Only then did she become aware of Benson and the snorting of the two greys in the stalls next to the Professor's.

Benson straightened, grooming brush in hand.

"He's taken a shine to you," Benson said in surprise. "He don't normally like strangers. What can I do for..." He voice trailed off as she turned to face him, and he frowned at her, uncomprehending, no doubt, as to why she should look so much like Ape the stable lad.

Now Benson had to look at her different, too. *Bloody viscount and his stupid ideas.*

She tilted her chin and met Benson's gaze with defiance. "I'm April," she said. "I'm his lordship's assistant."

"Are you?" Benson said slowly. "You look like Ape to me."

He couldn't have said anything that pleased her more, so there was no reason for the sudden tightening of her throat.

"I feel like Ape," she muttered. "But I've always been April."

"And himself found out?"

It was April's belief that himself had always known but had gone along with the charade at first because he hadn't much cared about anything. "Something like that. I'd rather stay with the horses. But I suppose they've got lots of grooms here already."

"There's a head groom and a lad. And a coachman. And now me."

Leaving the Professor, she petted each of the greys and allowed Benson to introduce her to the other horses, who must have been left over from the old viscount's day: a huge, black horse, a smaller chestnut mare, a shaggy old pony, and two, large carriage horses.

A shadow fell over her and she turned quickly, poised from instinct to bolt. But it was only the younger of the two grooms she had seen outside, staring at her.

"Jem," Benson said by way of introduction. "He's the stable lad. April's his lordship's assistant."

The boy's eyes were bold, both admiring and contemptuous. In St. Giles, she'd have kept out of his way. Here...

"I'll bet she is," Jem sneered. "Care to assist anyone else?"

April's cheeks burned with anger, against Petteril as much as against this oaf. She'd *told* him what people would think and say...

"April here saved his lordship's life, back in London," Benson said, apparently casual, although April could tell he was anything but. "A man's grateful for a service like that. So grateful he's liable to dismiss without a character anyone who speaks to her, or about her, with *any* disrespect. Especially what she ain't earned."

Jem muttered something—it might have been an apology—and went to fetch the water bucket.

Although secretly touched by Benson's defence, April realized it made any quick, easy friendships with the rest of the staff impossible. In the London house, she had been there before the rest of the staff and they had accepted her along with his lordship's other eccentricities, such as teaching reading to any who wished it. Here, she came to an established staff who had looked after the house for years. Her peculiar position of "assistant", with a room separate from the other maids, separated her from everyone else. Her place in the usual order of things was not clear. She had the special protection of his lordship. Inevitably, this caused resentment and suspicion.

When she went with some dread to the servants' hall, she was regarded with curiosity but no warmth. No one was rude, but no one was friendly either.

When, without thought, she took her place at the foot of the long table, which she was used to, Mrs. Hicks spoke sharply from the head of the table: "Up here, since you're placed above everyone else."

Mrs. Park in London had tried to explain to her the rigid hierarchy of domestic servants. It had seemed nonsensical to April, who didn't care where she sat as long as she ate, or who gave her orders providing she was paid and wasn't interfered with.

So, she rose from her lowly place and took the chair indicated beside the cook, Mrs. Drake, who sat beside Mrs. Hicks herself. Opposite them, on the other side of the housekeeper sat Stewart the valet.

No one spoke to April, not even Mrs. Drake or Mavis the upper housemaid on her other side. She was excluded, which made her feel just a little lonely after the acceptance of Mr. and Mrs. Park in London. But she was used to loneliness and refused to let it trouble her.

Besides which, it was interesting watching the other London servants. Benson was not head groom here, but he had the importance of looking after his lordship's favourite horses. Stewart, the silent valet was deferred to with the utmost politeness for here he was the top-ranking male servant, which he accepted with equal civility, somehow giving the impression that he would not throw his weight around unless he was displeased. For a man who said so little, he could convey a great deal during one quick meal.

Inevitably, the subject of the dead cove came up.

"Here, do you know Mr. Lindon was over here?" one of the maids whispered to the girl nearest her, though the conversations around her cut off like a tap and everyone gazed expectantly at the whispering maid, whose expression changed from wide-eyed curiosity to alarm.

"Calling on his lordship to welcome him home, as is only proper," Mrs. Hicks said dampingly.

"The very day he arrives?" the whispering maid said, apparently finding her courage. "I heard as his lordship found a corpse in the wood on his way home, and asked Mr. Lindon to call on him, being the magistrate. And that's why he came and why they went off together."

"Well, if his lordship found a corpse, so did *she*," the other maid said, jerking her head in April's direction.

Everyone gazed at April, who carried on eating her lemon sponge cake and custard.

"Who was it?" someone asked her.

"Was it horrible?" asked someone else.

April decided she should answer. "No one seems to know who he was. And no—it wasn't very nice but not horrible neither."

"Weren't you scared?" wondered the whispering maid with a shudder.

April blinked. "No. He were dead."

She foresaw a deluge of questions and laid down her spoon, prepared to make a dignified exit—or bolt if necessary—but Mrs. Hicks put a stop to it all by saying severely, "That will be more than enough on a topic not suitable for the table. If the poor soul wasn't known to anyone, you've no cause to be interested. Now..."

The housekeeper took a deep breath. "While you're all together, I've got a message to relay from his lordship, who is a scholar as well as a gentleman. And he is kindly prepared to teach reading and writing to any of you who missed out on school or just want to better yourself. Male and female servants are offered this chance, outside staff as well as inside. Whoever chooses to do it will be released from their duties for one hour at nine in the morning. But there's no skiving. He'll spot you and send you back to me."

There was utter silence, as all the servants looked at each other with amazement and doubt.

"Where does this lesson happen, then, Mrs. Hicks?" asked Mavis, and April realized with some indignation that they doubted Lord Petteril's motives.

"In the library," Mrs. Hicks said. Her mouth was tight. She was doing her duty, reporting Petteril's offer, but for whatever reason, she did not approve of it.

Across the table, Stewart stirred. "He offered the same to his London staff."

"I took him up on it," Benson said from the lower half of the table where the outside staff sat. "And I'll be continuing since the offer's there."

"What do we need to read for?" one of the smaller maids asked with dread.

"You don't need to," Mrs. Drake the cook said. "But it helps. I couldn't learn new recipes if I couldn't read, nor tell the price of ingredients. You'll never be a lady's maid let alone a decent cook or a housekeeper if you can't read. Same goes for any staff with responsibility."

"I'll be there," April said firmly.

"You?" one of the maids uttered, gawping at her. "You can't even read?"

April felt her cheeks burn, but she lifted her chin and stared the girl down. "I can now." Just. Long words and words that didn't follow normal pronunciation rules still gave her difficulty. And compared with Lord Petteril, she was painfully slow.

At the foot of the table, the gardener's boy snorted. He seemed about to make some jeering comment to April when somehow he caught Stewart's eye and lapsed into flustered silence.

"Well, don't just sit there, get on!" Mrs. Hicks commanded, and the sound of scraping chairs and muttered voices filled the hall.

April rose, took her dishes to the scullery as the others did, then sailed upstairs and through the baize door to the main house, as though she had every right.

She was fairly sure she would find Lord Petteril in the library, and she did. He sat at one of the tables, surrounded by large books and heaps of paper. He was wearing his spectacles, which he needed for reading, but which made the rest of his vision blurry.

He looked up somewhat owlishly. "April."

"They know I'm still learning to read," she said without preamble. "So no one will believe I'm your secretary."

"Assistant," he corrected, distractedly.

"And you think they're not debating what I assist you with?"

He stared at her and she stared back, determined not to give in to the sudden shame heating her face and neck.

He sighed and took off the spectacles. "Talk is inevitable. It will die down when nothing feeds it. Your situation is unusual. It is not illegal or immoral. Would you rather go to Lady Haggard?"

Lady Haggard was the stepmother of his friend, Sir Peter. April had never met her, but she was prepared to take April in while she "practised" being a girl again. A kind offer and perfectly appropriate of Lord Petteril to bring it up again when April had made her unhappiness clear. Yet for some reason, it infuriated her.

"No," she snapped and stalked out.

SHE WAS AWARE, AS SHE stormed up the stairs, that she was being totally unreasonable. Moreover, addressing her employer in such a way was grounds for dismissal without a character. In her heart she knew he had done more for her than she had ever dreamed anyone would or could, and he did not deserve her temper. Yet his kindness was unbearable because it came with the nasty little suspicions of others, dirtying the very odd but necessary friendship between them. How had she come to rely on that so quickly?

Because she had been lonely, and never admitted it even to herself. Because he had vulnerabilities only she knew about it, and he trusted her. In London, she had thought of it as a mutual reliance. Here, he was so much more lord of the manor and she the servant in the ambiguous position.

She threw open the door of the chamber he had insisted she have. Mrs. Hicks had shown her it and she had left her bag here, but her mind had been elsewhere. Only now did she appreciate the wonder of having a room of her own.

Petteril House in London had been a haven of safety, a mattress on the kitchen floor, then a straw bed in the stables with the warm smell of horses in her nostrils, or a corner of Benson's room when it was too cold or wet. This was...opulence.

A proper bed, a chest of drawers to keep her clothes, a stuffed chair, a wash stand with a water jug and bowl and a bar of soap. Another upright chair by a slightly wobbly little desk. And a window, with curtains.

Her throat ached. This was the room of a trusted servant. It had belonged to the nurse who had cared for Lord Petteril's cousins. April had never had a place of her own, a place to keep her things. Well, she had never had any things. Now she had clothes, a carpet bag, a purse Lord Petteril had given her with her first pay.

She had had a job then, caring for the horses. What the hell was she was supposed to do as his assistant? Sit here and twiddle her thumbs, appreciating her luxury and her good fortune?

She opened the bag with unnecessary force and put her clothes away in drawers. A few chemises, stockings, two spare dresses cut down and made for her in secret by Mrs. Park. A few white caps, a bonnet suitable for a maid's day off. The cloak she had travelled in. The outdoor, leather boots. And at the bottom, another bar of the sweet-smelling soap that she loved, a hair brush, a tooth brush and powder. And her purse, and the book Lord Petteril had given her to read.

She turned and caught her reflection in the slightly spotted mirror on the chest of drawers. She stared at the unfamiliar vision somewhat dubiously.

Well, if you're the assistant, she told herself, *learn to assist.*

She picked up the book and notebook and took them to the desk, where a bottle of ink already sat in a stand with a quill pen and a knife to trim it. A small tray of sand to blot the writings.

She sat down and opened her book where she had marked it. Painfully, she read the whole page, then, even more painfully, set about copying it out in ink.

Chapter Four

The first night of his return to Haybury Court as its lord, Piers did not sleep well. His mind spun around the interlinking problems of the murdered corpse, the estate, and April, and would not be still. He finally drifted into uneasy slumber, but sprang into wakefulness as usual at first light.

As was his custom, he washed and shaved himself before dressing in riding attire and heading downstairs. He caused a flurry in the servants' hall by wandering into the kitchen in search of coffee.

Two yawning maids clutched each other in horror and the scullery maid dropped a large pan with a clatter.

"Mr. Piers, you should ring for what you want!" the cook scolded, bustling in from the pantry with a scowl. "You're upsetting the maids. What can we get for you?"

"A cup of coffee if you please," he said humbly, and rather to his surprise, she smiled at him.

"Bless you, my lord, go back upstairs and we'll bring it. A slice of toast? Breakfast?"

"Not yet, just the coffee."

A word from Cookie, as he and his cousins had always called her, sent the maids into action. Following a remembered trail from his childhood, Piers wandered out the back door to sniff the air and test the temperature, before returning to claim his coffee.

"You were always stubborn," Cookie remarked.

"Was I?" he said in surprise, taking a grateful sip from the steaming cup.

"In your own quiet way."

He smiled amiably and strolled back outside. Cup in hand, he sauntered around the kitchen garden and then around the perimeter of the house, taking mental notes while he walked and drank. Abandoning his cup on the bench outside the kitchen door, he ambled round to the stables. Benson, used to his habits, was already up and about though there was no sign of the head groom or the lad.

"Morning, my lord. Want the Professor saddled?" Benson asked cheerfully.

Piers stroked the Professor's snorting nose, and his ears, and gave him the biscuit he had found in his coffee saucer. "He's had a long journey," Piers said, "I think I should give him a day of rest, don't you?"

"I would advise it," Benson said, "but a short ride probably wouldn't hurt."

"Hmm." Piers moved on past the greys, to whom he murmured nonsense, and a couple of carriage horses who seemed a bit under the weather. The mare and the large hunter seemed somewhat subdued also,

"They're bored," Benson said. "No one's exercised them properly for years. Just kept them clean and fed and walked around the yard."

Piers frowned.

"Jem, the boy, can't ride," Benson explained. "And Mr. Carter, the head groom has a bad leg where he got kicked by some stallion of his late lordship's."

"I see. Let's saddle the hunter. Does he have a name?"

"Not that they've told me."

"Orion," Piers decided somewhat optimistically since the beast didn't appear much like a hunting god right now.

Orion walked out placidly enough, though he shifted restlessly, pulling up his head when Benson put the saddle on his back. They gave him time to get used to it again before fastening it on. He snorted and danced with annoyance while Piers mounted him and Benson adjusted the stirrups, but he seemed keen enough to move forward.

The morning was fresh and bright, promising a fair day. Piers felt his spirits lift, away from the anxiety of last night which had got out of proportion as it often did. He would keep to his morning rides here. The memories bombarding him were far from all bad—long summers spent in games with Ivor, his brother, and his cousins John and George and Bertie. Sometimes Maria was there, too, and even the small, much younger, happy child that Gussie had been. They had all played and quarrelled, laughed together and occasionally fought.

Things had changed, of course, as they had grown older and learned about precedence, that George would be Lord Petteril one day, and Piers, youngest and weakest, was more obviously, the runt of the family litter. Girls didn't count. Piers had never been sure if he had become more annoying, or if his cousins were stretching their authority muscles. Either way, their turning on him had hurt, although not so much as when his own brother took their side and joined in.

After that, summers here, visits to Petteril House in London, were no longer much fun. Piers had withdrawn and gone his own way towards scholarship with a determination that verged on the obsessive. Which of course, had confirmed the other boys' belief in his contemptible weakness.

And yet, of the male cousins, only Bertie and Piers still lived. And Piers was Viscount Petteril after all.

Orion perked at first, delighted to stretch his legs in a full, if short gallop. But he was quickly winded. It would take some time to get him fit again, and a few consultations with the head groom. What was his name? Carter? Piers didn't remember him from the old days. He must be relatively new. Though there had been several grooms in Piers's boyhood. He could easily be one of them promoted.

Over-promoted, Piers suspected. He was still mulling this as Orion carried him slowly home, joining the path that linked Haybury Court to Lindon Grange. Here, he was surprised to see Mr. Lindon cantering toward him on a fine bay.

"Mr. Lindon!" Piers called in surprise. "Beautiful morning, is it not? Somehow, I had not taken you for an early riser!"

"Oh, I'm not," Lindon replied fervently, reining in beside him. "Keeping clear of the family because I'm afraid to tell them."

"Tell them what?" Piers asked, focusing on the man's genuine distress.

"I had news from the Dog and Duck on the London road," Lindon replied miserably. "Apparently Lord Maxwell Hunter stayed there on Monday night but according to the ostler my fellow spoke to, he left early without anyone seeing him. Didn't even pay his shot."

"Even though you didn't expect him until Wednesday? Perhaps he went to visit a friend first. He wasn't obliged to give his entire itinerary to the innkeeper, let alone the ostler." Piers frowned. "Besides, you saw they body. Wouldn't you know him?" Unless Lindon suffered the same affliction as Piers where faces were concerned...

"Well, no, I wouldn't," Lindon said, raking his fingers through his hair and knocking his hat askew. "That's the whole point. My wife and daughter met him last winter at a party at her cousin's house. I didn't go. And most correspondence between us since then has been conducted through our men of business."

Piers blinked. "Men of business? Were you in some kind of dispute with Hunter?"

"Lord no, he wants to marry my daughter! That's why he was coming here, now the settlements are agreed. Dear God, what a terrible tragedy. To have him murdered, only miles from our door, and now I will have to tell his family somehow..."

"You can't yet jump to such conclusions," Piers soothed. "Even if he did leave the Dog and Duck in the middle of the night instead of the morning, the man had no reason to be in Petteril Wood, did he?"

"No," Lindon agreed. "But he's the only young gentleman reported to have stayed at any of the inns within riding distance of us. None of our neighbours have lost visitors or expected anyone who hasn't turned up. It has to be Hunter, but only my wife and Laura would be able to identify the corpse and you'll understand that I hesitate to ask them!"

"Yes, of course," Piers agreed. "But surely someone else of your household? One of the servants, perhaps?"

"I've asked," Lindon said gloomily. "None of them had anything to do with him. Oscar met him, of course, for he escorted his mother and sister to the party, but he won't be home until later. I suppose I must wait until then to clear the matter up."

"I suppose you must."

"And in the meantime, I don't want to let something slip to Evangela or Laura."

"Come and have breakfast, if you like. After that, I'm tied up for most of the day."

"Are you? Evangela was hoping you would come and take tea," Lindon said gloomily. "No doubt to impress Hunter with our other aristocratic friends."

"If the settlements are agreed, surely you have no further need to impress him?" Piers said, then added hastily, "but of course I will come for tea if you wish it. Hopefully, by then Oscar will have come home and told you the body is not Lord Maxwell's."

IT WAS ALMOST NINE by the time Piers managed to persuade Lindon from the house, duly fed and awash with tea. Having forced himself not to enquire for her, he was relieved to find April in the library, along with Benson, Jem the stable-lad, and one of the maids whose name was Nell. April had set each place with slates, chalk and pencils, and found his stash of notebooks to provide them for Jem and Nell.

Having bade April and Benson continue with their reading for now, he spent most of his time teaching the letters and the sounds they made to his new students. Then he wrote their names for them, and bade them copy them several times, which gave him time to hear Benson and April's reading.

He felt a warm glow to realize they had both been practising. And in their writing, April in particular had begun to form her letters with much more confidence and even elegance.

There was no sign in April of last night's anger, and she had dressed properly for the day. She even smelled good, which was a direction he could not allow his thought to wander. And after the lesson, she lingered to put things away.

"I'll be with the estate steward for much of the day," he informed her.

"What are my duties?" she asked, expressionlessly.

"I'd like you to begin with the public rooms. Go round them all and note what you think needs to be done. Complete redecoration, furniture or carpets replaced, curtains needing mending or thrown out, that kind of thing. Make a note of each, so that you remember."

She seemed to perk at this, although just as he was sure she was about to smile, she said, "Is that not Mrs. Hicks's job?"

"No, it's yours. Mrs. Hicks has enough to do." He hesitated, rubbing his forehead with the side of his hand, then let his arm fall to his side. "I'd like to go back to the woods, to where we found the body. Do you want to come?"

"Yes," she said at once. "Why, though?"

"I'm not sure. I don't think I paid enough attention at the time. Do you remember seeing bloodstains anywhere at the clearing? Apart from under the body?"

She frowned, not with disgust but with the effort of memory. "No, I didn't notice."

"And it's been raining since then, but you never know. Something might remain, or some other clue we and the constables both missed. Oh, and Mr. Lindon thinks our man might be Lord Maxwell Hunter after all. Apparently he left a nearby inn to come here, probably very early on Tuesday, and hasn't been seen since. And the man's engaged to Laura, Lindon's daughter."

"Oh dear."

"Indeed. Our best hope is that Oscar Lindon comes home to identify his lordship as soon as possible."

AFTER A GRUELLING SEVERAL hours with Sullivan Daniels, his uncle's and now his own land steward, Piers understood how little he knew. He had not been brought up to care for the land. His own father's land should have gone to Ivor, and Piers's interests had been much less practical. Despite his best efforts, he could not learn a lifetime's experience and all the new methods of farming from books and ledgers. Accordingly, he arranged to ride out with Daniels on the following several days, both to inspect the land and meet his tenants.

With some relief, he sent for April at about three of the clock and ordered his uncle's carriage horses harnessed to the curricle – both as an experiment and to give the greys a well-earned rest.

Just as he climbed into the curricle, April came flying around the corner, her cloak clutched under one arm, and a leather pouch attached to a girdle at her waist. It was just the right size for her notebook.

"I made it," she said proudly of the pouch. "From an old bag and a girdle they were throwing out."

"Ingenious," Piers said. "And very useful. Up you come. The horses are quite excited to be in harness again."

All the way to the woods, she chattered, much as she had in London, bouncing from topic to topic, including the corpse, his missing boots and possessions, the names and states of various rooms in Haybury Court, and what Piers's favourite colours were.

"You don't forget places, do you?" she said, when he pulled the horses to a standstill on the road through the woods. "I'd never have found this spot again." She jumped down and tied the reins around the same tree Piers had used the day before and walked beside him toward the clearing where they had found the corpse.

There was nothing left of the fire except a few bits of charred wood around the outside edges. They scrutinized the whole clearing between them. Then, Piers leaned his shoulder against a tree. April, crouching at his feet like the urchin she was, looked up at him.

"There's only blood where he fell," she remarked. "So they didn't fight."

"There's no other sign of a fight either," Piers said. "The ground's not churned up, and it's only flattened where our man was lying. No footprints. No hoof prints. No wheel marks. How the devil did either of them get here?"

"Rain must have washed them away. There's no sign we were ever here neither."

"True. So why would Hunter have come here in the first place?"

April considered. "Assignation with Miss Lindon?"

"Possible. Only I get the impression it is a marriage of convenience and Laura hasn't seen him since they met at some party in the winter. Lindon hasn't even met him."

"Do you suppose she wants to marry him?" April wondered. "Maybe she did him in to avoid it."

Piers jaw dropped. "Extreme. Lindon isn't a monster. I'm sure a simple *No* would have stopped the marriage without resorting to murder. Besides, would she really have gone to meet him alone? At night? In my woods?"

"Doesn't seem very likely," April admitted reluctantly. "Though it would explain why there was no fight. He wouldn't expect a young lady to chib him." Her frown deepened into a scowl. "That's a point, though. Why would anyone come to your land? Except that it's empty. Pretty much."

"Apart from the odd poacher. Daniels has scared off a few, but not in the last few weeks. Also, I don't know anything about this Maxwell Hunter, except that his father must be a marquis or a duke." Piers straightened. "Which is a pretty good catch for the squire's daughter. Why did Hunter pick her if it wasn't a love match?"

"Is she rich?" April asked cynically.

"Not by a duke's standards. Or even his younger sons' standards. Come on, let's go and have tea at Lindon Grange."

"Want me to sit at the back of the drawing room and take notes?" April asked cheekily, jumping up and trotting beside him out of the clearing. "Mrs. L. will hardly notice me."

"No, I want you to go the kitchen and see what you can ferret out from the servants."

"You think it was one of them? Or one of the family?"

"I can't see why any of the Lindons' servants would kill a nobleman they had bever seen. Or why any of the Lindons would—er... do in such a fine match for Laura."

"Maybe he's horrible. Maybe he betrayed her."

Piers glanced down at her in surprise. "Would it feel like betrayal? After one meeting several months ago?"

"Doesn't have to be betrayed love," she said, colour seeping into her face. "You nobs seem more concerned with your own pride and appearance."

"Sadly true," Piers said, brushing a speck of dirt off his coat. "Have I acquired the appearance of the perfect country gentleman?"

"Be proud, mister."

"Insolence," Piers said, climbing back into the curricle while April untied the reins from the tree, "will be punished."

"By most nobs," April allowed, handing him the reins. "You seem more pleased by it than not."

"Do I?" he said in surprise as she hurried round the back of the curricle and jumped up beside him. "I expect it depends on the particular insolence."

Although he had not been there for seven years, Piers remembered the way to Lindon Grange quite easily. He was more thrown by the gaggle of people who had apparently spilled out of the front door of the house. Beyond distinguishing two men and three women, he was utterly thrown.

"Mrs. Lindon in the purple dress now," April murmured. "Her daughter's in pink. Mr. Lindon has more hair than the other cove and I've no idea who he or the older mort is."

Piers felt warmth suffuse his face, not just with embarrassment or relief, but because April's low, matter-of-fact provision of information spoke of acceptance. And was just what he needed. There was no time even to glance at her, for everyone around the door had turned to gaze at him and smile.

April scrambled down to the horses' heads, and he alighted in what he thought of as his viscount role.

"Mrs. Lindon," he said, smiling at his hostess even before she moved to greet him. "I hope you don't mind my informal call." He bowed to her and to the others. "Miss Lindon. Sir."

"Of course we are delighted, my lord," Mrs. Lindon said warmly. "Allow me to present Mr. and Mrs. Vernon. Mr. Vernon is the vicar, who replaced Mr. Jenkins."

"How do you do?" Piers said, bowing to both.

"Oh my, so delighted to meet you, my lord. We did not know quite what to expect, but so very...I'm sure...charmed..." Mrs. Vernon fluttered into incoherence, and her husband cast her a glance of irritation.

"Lord Petteril," he said loudly, perhaps to cover up his wife's half-lost murmurings. "Glad to see you taking up your duties. Haybury

Court has been deserted for too long. The people need a gentleman of duty and godliness to provide example. The Lord does not like fashionable fribbles."

Piers blinked. "I hope I am not a fribble."

"Oh, my goodness, no," Mrs. Vernon murmured. "So perfect a gentleman..."

"Come, Mrs. Vernon," the vicar boomed. "Time we were about our own duties. I look forward to seeing you on Sunday, my lord. Mrs. Lindon, our thanks. Goodbye."

He marched over to the gig and pony which Piers had just driven past. Mrs. Vernon trotted after him, twittering thanks and delight over her shoulder. A groom waited at the pony's head, quick to throw the reins to Mr. Vernon, who hadn't waited to hand in his wife first. It was the groom who did that before striding over to April at the curricle.

"Come inside, my lord," Mrs. Lindon said graciously. "We'll have some fresh tea."

"Thank you," Piers murmured. The groom was leading the horses around toward the stables now, April walking beside him and chattering. Which made Piers want to smile.

"Oscar is home and very much looking forward to meeting you," Mrs. Lindon told him with a smile, leading the way across the handsome hall, which was much as Piers remembered it, and into a gracious drawing room.

Before following her, Piers paused to raise his eyebrows at Lindon. "Has Oscar seen...?"

"Not yet," Lindon said unhappily. "I couldn't insist with his mother so glad to see him and Laura on tenterhooks for Hunter to turn up. I can't bring myself to tell them."

There was no time for more. Walking into the drawing room, Piers was reintroduced to Oscar Lindon, whom he remembered as a serious boy, happy enough to get into mischief providing he didn't get dirty at the same time. At the time Piers had blamed the influence of his mother for such fastidiousness.

Now, he met a man a few inches shorter than himself but very neatly and properly dressed in a well-fitting coat and shining shoes. There were no obvious signs of recent travel except a certain tiredness around the eyes. Oscar was fairer than the rest of the family, but he had his father's nose and something of his mother's proud posture. Although not particularly handsome, at surely only eight or nine and twenty, he was already distinguished.

"My lord," he said to Piers, bowing and advancing with a smile. "How good to see you!"

Piers offered his hand and had it warmly shaken. "And you, but please don't *my lord* me. It sounds wrong when you were the one who hauled me out of the river like a drowned rat after I fell out of that tree."

"Did I?" Oscar sounded surprised.

"I expect he complained because you got him wet, too," Laura said.

"Do you know, I believe he did," Piers agreed, smiling. "But I was so grateful not to be dead that I didn't care."

"Boys will be boys," Lindon said jovially. "Sit down, Petteril."

"We heard you had devoted yourself to study at Oxford," Oscar said, taking a seat beside Piers. "It must have been quite a shock to be flung back into the world."

More than you will ever know. "It still is," Piers said mildly. "I'm slowly finding my feet."

"Are you fixed here for some time, then?"

"For a couple of weeks at least. Probably until the end of the month. It rather depends on what I learn from Daniels over the next few days. There are other estates, too, though smaller."

Oscar nodded. "Of course. And I gather there is much to do. Daniels found it difficult to interest his late lordship in the land. Everyone was delighted to hear you were coming. In fact, hopefully you will still be here for Laura's wedding."

Laura blushed. "Oscar! He is not even here yet, so you must not assume—"

To Piers, her protest sounded a curiously discordant note, which may have been what caused her brother to interrupt.

"I assure you we would take it very ill if our assumptions proved wrong," he said dryly. "Such a fuss over settlements! You will find the same, Petteril, when you marry."

"I have much to see to before that happy day," Piers said.

Oscar smiled. "As do I."

Piers turned to Laura. "You are engaged to Lord Maxwell Hunter, I believe? I don't think we have met."

"He is the Marquis of Aylesworth's son," Mrs. Lindon said proudly.

"Fourth son," Laura added, which made her mother frown in annoyance. "Otherwise, I daresay, he would never have considered me."

"I don't see why not," Oscar said sharply. "Your family may not be titled, but you are as gently born as he is. There have Lindons at the Grange since the Conquest. Before, probably."

"You need not jump to my defence," Laura said with a quick smile. "I quite understand the way of the world."

"I wish you very happy," Piers said. "How did you meet?"

"Oh, at a cousin's party in Oxfordshire. Mama and Oscar and I went to stay for several days, and Lord Maxwell was one of the other guests." She glanced at him and seemed to think something more was called for. "He is very handsome and has charming manners."

Which was rather faint praise for one's future husband. Piers began to wonder what was wrong with him. What *had* been wrong with him before someone stuck a hunting knife in his heart.

"I have brought Laura up to be a modest young lady," Mrs. Lindon intervened, taking charge of the teapot which had just been brought in. "Though I don't think she need be quite so modest about her future husband."

As she spoke, Piers heard the sound outside of wheels on gravel. Laura heard it, too, for she stiffened, one arm stealing across her stomach in a gesture that spoke to him of self-protection. Well, a young lady had much to fear from a relative stranger who was suddenly put in charge of everything she did and everything she had.

"Ah, that should be Lord Maxwell," Mrs. Lindon said comfortably.

Piers looked at Lindon who shifted uncomfortably in his chair, and at Oscar, who drew in his breath, almost like girding up his loins for confrontation. Piers received his tea from Laura, whose fingers trembled slightly. He hoped it *would* be Lord Maxwell, though that would leave even more of a mystery as to the identity of the dead man.

Voices sounded in the hall, muffled and indistinguishable, and then the drawing room door opened.

"Mrs. Alleyn, and Mr. Samuel Alleyn," announced the butler.

Laura relaxed. Lindon looked at Piers with a sort of conspiratorial resignation, as though this were the final proof they needed.

Mrs. Lindon looked annoyed, as though she knew her unexpected visitors had come to gawp, though whether at Piers or at Laura's husband-to-be, he could not tell. Like all the gentlemen, Piers rose to his feet as a broad-boned, plump and stocky lady sailed into the room, rather like his aunt Hortensia except that he read only good humour in this lady's face.

"Alleyn's in trade," Oscar murmured to Piers with distaste. "But since they are our neighbours over at Barnwood, we are obliged to receive them."

"How kind of you to call," Mrs. Lindon was saying to the plump lady, with a curious mixture of condescension and graciousness. "Allow me to present you to our guest. My lord, our neighbour Mrs. Alleyn, and her son, Mr. Samuel Alleyn. Viscount Petteril, of course."

Mrs. Alleyn beamed at him, not a whit awed by his title. "How do you do, sir? Very pleased to meet you." She spoke with a slightly northern accent that betrayed her origins.

Piers bowed. "And I you, ma'am." He turned to her son, an upright, if slightly awkward looking young man, probably a year or so younger than himself. He was quite good looking, though he held himself very stiffly. Piers hoped it was not from embarrassment at his mother or the unkind condescension of his hosts.

Piers offered him one casual hand, and Samuel looked somewhat surprised, though he shook it with firmness. "Pleased to meet another neighbour," Piers said.

"My lord." Piercing blue eyes searched Piers's face as though looking for hidden insult. Finding none, Samuel gave a very small smile before turning to bow to Laura. "Miss Lindon."

"Good day, Mr. Alleyn," Laura said with a pleasant smile. "I hope you are well?"

"Perfectly, thank you." Deeper colour seeped into his face. He cast a sweeping glance about the room, adding awkwardly, "And you, Miss Lindon?"

"Oh yes, as always!" Laura sat and arranged her skirts once more as though desperately seeking a topic of conversation. Or just a distraction from her betrothed's continued absence. "Do sit down, Mr. Alleyn. Have you heard the latest news? Lord Petteril found a dead body in his wood!"

"So it is true?" Mrs. Alleyn exclaimed. "And is it truly a stranger?"

"It would seem so," Lindon said, crossing then uncrossing his legs and shifting in his chair. "No one has recognized him."

Samuel threw a frown at him. "So that is why you were asking me about expected visitors?"

"Afraid so," Lindon admitted. "I have to ask everyone, as magistrate, you understand."

"Poor soul, how awful," Mrs. Alleyn said with genuine sympathy, presumably for the corpse. "And for your lordship, of course, to have come across such a thing almost as soon as you're home."

"When would be a better time, Mrs. Alleyn?" Mrs. Lindon asked glacially.

"Oh, I never, I suppose." Mrs. Alleyn did not appear to take offence although her son's lips tightened. "It just seems the worst possible. I suppose the best we can hope now is that Mr. Lindon here discovers who he is and returns him to his grieving family. So sad." She turned to Oscar. "And so, you are returned from your adventures. I trust you had a pleasant trip?"

"Indeed, but it was hardly an adventure, merely a meeting with friends," Oscar replied. He spoke with courtesy, but it was chilly. The Alleyns, clearly, were never allowed to forget that they were beneath the ranks of the gentry. No wonder Samuel was so tense. It must make visiting intolerable.

Although, he began to suspect another reason for Samuel's discomfort over the next few minutes, as conversation flowed, breaking into several smaller ones. Samuel sat beside Laura, speaking earnestly, although the glow in his eyes betrayed that he was hopelessly smitten. And she betrothed to another man. Admittedly a dead one, but—

The drawing room door opened again, and the butler intoned, "Lord Maxwell Hunter, ma'am."

Chapter Five

P iers was fairly sure his jaw dropped, though fortunately no one was looking at him. Everyone jerked their gaze toward the door, whether in astonishment, pleasure, or avid curiosity.

"Oh, thank God," Lindon muttered, while his wife's shoulders relaxed and she went forward with a beaming smile on her face. She might have believed the corpse was not Lord Maxwell, but she still had not been sure he would come.

On Laura he seemed to have the opposite effect. Colour surged into her cheeks, and her fingers gripped each other so hard they looked white. Samuel Alleyn stood slowly, as though unwilling to meet the man who had cut him out merely by birth.

Lord Maxwell had strolled into the room and came to a startled halt to find so much attention fixed to him. "Oh, Lord, did I wear the wrong coat?" It wasn't even a sneer, or any kind of sarcasm, merely a self-deprecating amusement that was oddly charming.

Mrs. Lindon laughed, giving her hand. "Of course not! How funny you are. Welcome to Lindon Grange, Lord Maxwell."

He bowed over her hand with enviable grace. "Thank you. I am delighted to be here! I did mean to arrive earlier in the day, but I had no one reliable to wake me. Miss Lindon, how delightful you look. Did I tell you once you should always blue? Now I think you should always wear pink."

Laura smiled nervously, offering her hand, which he gallantly kissed, his eyes smiling lazily at her with what Piers recognized as practised and probably habitual flirtation.

Behind her, Oscar had come up to shake his hand. "Welcome, my lord! You have not yet my father, have you? Mr. Robert Lindon."

Lord Maxwell turned to Lindon with an easy blend of courtesy and respect. "Sir, an honour to meet you at last."

"Likewise, my lord, likewise," Lindon said, perhaps a little too jovially, but he was clearly elated that the corpse was not Lord Maxwell after all. "Allow me to present our other guests, our neighbours, Mrs. Alleyn and Lord Petteril. And Mr. Samuel Alleyn, of course."

Lord Maxwell bowed civilly to the Alleyns, his smile still in place, before turning to Piers with rather more genuine interest. His smile broadened. "Petteril, eh? I was desolate not to meet you in London. You caused quite a stir."

"I did?" Piers said, startled. He clasped the offered hand.

"Well, you defied expectations. Instead of a carelessly dressed and bespectacled academic, they beheld the next best thing to a dandy, witty and cultured and yet fashionably aloof. With a bang up set of greys to pull his smart curricle, and a small tiger enviably fluent in thieves' cant to ride up behind. Naturally, I was agog to meet you, so this is an unexpected pleasure."

"Naturally," Piers said. "You are enviably fluent yourself."

Lord Maxwell laughed. "You mean I prattle finest balderdash? Behold me nervous in the presence of beauty." He threw his charming smile toward Laura and Samuel Alleyn's lips twisted.

"Mother," Samuel said, "It's time we left our hosts to their guest."

"Of course," Mrs. Alleyn said comfortably, allowing Samuel to haul her to her feet. She beamed at Lord Maxwell. "I'm sure the Lindons are doubly glad to see you, since you're obviously not the corpse in the wood!"

"Corpse?" Lord Maxwell's eyebrows flew up. "I hope not! Got a corpse on your hands, sir?"

"Robert is Justice of the Peace," Mrs. Lindon said, glaring at Mrs. Alleyn who looked abashed for the first time.

"Sorry," she murmured. "My tongue runs ahead of my brain. I don't mean to spoil your reunion."

"Come, Mother," Samuel said, pausing only to throw thanks at Mrs. Lindon, bow to the company in general and cast a last look at Laura before hustling his parent from the room.

Lord Maxwell allowed himself to be pressed into Samuel's vacant chair and accepted a cup of tea poured by his prospective mother in law and presented by his betrothed. But his frowning gaze was on Robert Lindon.

"Did you really think the corpse was me?"

"No, no, of course not," Lindon said, flustered, then, "Well, it crossed my mind."

"Why?"

Since this seemed to flummox Lindon, Piers answered. "It was the body of a young man about your age and build, unknown to anyone in the village, and clearly a man of means and leisure. Someone at the Dog and Duck said you had left very early on Tuesday to come to the Grange. Our man died probably in the small hours of Tuesday morning."

"Did he, by God?" Hunter said slowly. He set down his cup and looked from Piers to Lindon. "Do you still not know who he is?"

"Haven't a clue," Lindon admitted.

Hunter's lips twisted. "I might have. You'd better take me to look."

TEN MINUTES LATER, Piers was back in the curricle with April and following the Lindon coach down the drive to the village road.

"Well, if it ain't him," April said, "Who does he think it is?"

"He didn't say."

"Are we going back to the Red Lion with them?"

"Oh, I think so," Piers said vaguely. "What did you learn from the servants?"

"That this Lord Maxwell is a nob of the first order and a fine catch for Miss Laura. Only his pockets're all to let and he's clearly after her for her money. They hope he appreciates her for more than her readies."

Piers raised his eyebrows. "I'd no idea the Lindons were so wealthy."

"They're not. Laura is. Inherited a fortune from some great aunt who married a nabob. It's hers when she marries."

Piers whistled. "Well discovered. Only if her fortune is so great, why don't they look higher? Maxwell is only a fourth son, never likely to be marquis unless the entire family is struck by plague. There must be an earl going spare, or even a duke on his last legs."

"Cynical cove, ain't you? Word is, the neighbour's son wants to marry her too. He's rich but beneath her. They're worried she'll take him over the nob."

"Him being Samuel Alleyn."

"That's the name. What's the matter?"

"I'm not convinced she wants to marry either of them," Piers said. "But she's a good daughter and will oblige her family."

"He looks well enough," April allowed. "Is he horrible?"

"No, he seems quite likeable, in a frivolous sort of way."

"Vice," April said with a sigh.

"What?"

"Vice. Young, frivolous nobs always have vice. Drink, gaming, brothels and not the cheap sort neither. We shouldn't let her marry him."

"We shouldn't?" Piers asked, fascinated.

"Not unless she's horrible, too."

"I don't think she is, though to be honest, I have no idea. Presumably her father and brother looked into Hunter's affairs, though."

"What, like your family looked into Henry Dove's?" April said scornfully, referring to his aunt Hortensia's efforts to marry his cousin Gussie to a fortune-hunting lout with nothing in his favour whatsoever except a plausible charm of manner.

"Fair point," Piers said. "I shall enquire."

Abandoning their slower horses in the Red Lion's yard, Piers and April were only just in time to follow Lindon and Hunter down to the cellar. The body lay where it had before, but this time there was no doctor to draw back the sheet.

Lindon hesitated, a natural fastidiousness showing in his face. Or perhaps it was superstition. Without a word, April brushed past him, drew the sheet down to the man's neck, and stood back.

Piers kept his gaze on Lord Maxwell and saw at once that he knew him. Even in the cellar's gloom, he could see the blood drain from Hunter's face, the wobble of his Adam's apple as he swallowed, his expression one of pity and regret. But he did not close his eyes.

"His name is Nathaniel Orr," he said quietly. "He is—was—my valet. I shall write to his family. How did he die?"

Lindon shuffled, perhaps looking for the right words to tell a man his closest servant had been so brutally done to death.

Piers had less qualms and more curiosity. "He was stabbed through the heart with a hunting knife."

Lord Maxwell dragged his gaze from the corpse to stare at Piers. "Good God." Astonishment, distaste, shock, and yet less of each than might be expected. "Who would do such a thing? Why?"

"We don't know yet," Piers answered. "Lindon is investigating, though it was harder when his identity was so difficult."

"I don't see why. He carried a letter of introduction from me as a matter of course, for ease in carrying out his duties. And there would have been other means of—"

"There was nothing, I assure you," Lindon said gravely.

"We found him naked, his clothes burned," Piers added.

Lord Maxwell blanched. "But that's barbaric! Damnable enough killing a man but why humiliate him?"

"Shall we discuss it outside?" Lindon suggested, hastening to the steps and leaving April to replace the sheet over the dead man's head.

Piers was as glad as the others to be out in the fresh air, which he breathed in with gratitude.

"Glass of brandy?" Lindon suggested, already charging toward the inn's front door.

"Might we have it out here?" Hunter asked. "I find my stomach isn't as strong as I thought, but it likes the open air."

Lindon nodded briskly, opened the door and simply yelled for Barnes. There was a wooden bench and a table to one side of the door, divided from the rest of the yard by a low wall. Piers and Lindon sat on the bench, Hunter fetched an abandoned stool and sat at one end of the table.

"Brandy," Lindon told the innkeeper who'd stuck his head out of the door. "And three mugs of ale."

"And a small beer," Piers added, nodding at April, who sat on the low wall a couple of feet away from the table, rummaging in her home made bag.

By silent consent, they waited until the maid set their drinks before them. She left the brandy bottle on the table.

Lindon tossed back half the brandy before him. "Any idea why your man Orr would have been in Petteril's wood in the middle of the night?" he asked Hunter

Hunter shook his head, swirling the brandy in his glass. "Nor at any other time."

Piers said, "Let's go back to the beginning. When did you last see him?"

Without any sign from him, April had taken her notebook and opened it on her lap. She held the pencil casually, as though she were comfortable with it. Four weeks ago, she couldn't write her own name.

"Monday afternoon in the Dog and Duck," Hunter was saying rue-fully. "I told him to have my things packed up ready to leave in the morning. Instead of which I had to pack my own *and* his." He sighed, and knocked back the brandy in one quick, practised motion. "I was going to dismiss him."

"Why?" Lindon pounced.

"I'm not an exacting master," Hunter said wryly, "but even I expect my orders to be carried out before a servant takes the leave I've just given him."

Lindon nodded sagely.

Piers asked, "Why did you give him leave when you were coming to Lindon Grange?"

Hunter frowned, an expression of annoyance crossing his face, oddly mixed with amusement. He glanced at Lindon, his prospective father-in-law and sighed. "I was going to stay with bachelor friends for a couple of nights and didn't want him with me."

From which Piers understood he was going off on a debauch that he didn't want getting back to the Lindons.

"I gave Orr two days leave and told him to be at Lindon Grange on Wednesday by midday." He smiled charmingly at Lindon. "I meant to be there myself by then, but as I explained, I was unavoidably detained."

By a thick head, Piers deduced, and no doubt some comely wench. Poor Laura Lindon.

Fortunately, Lindon's mind was clinging to the valet. "Why did he come here so early, then? He didn't even wait to pack your bags or his own, but came straight to this area two days early. It makes no sense."

"He packed *some* of his own stuff," Hunter offered. "He took his smaller bag, with his shaving kit and so on, but left the rest. I know because I noticed it was gone when I packed up *his* things."

Piers put down his glass. "He meant to return to the Dog and Duck."

"And travel twice to this area?" Lindon said doubtfully. "Why would he do that?"

"It's not that far, easily done for the young and fit," Piers mused. "Only, of course, we don't know how he travelled here. It would be a long walk. Could he ride?"

"Yes, he could," Hunter admitted, lifting his mug. "But he doesn't have a horse."

"Hiring one is easy enough. Presumably you left him enough money to travel with."

Hunter didn't dispute it. "Perhaps he had friends, or even family in the area, though he didn't mention any to me. It could have been a romantic assignation, I suppose."

Piers straightened. "Perhaps with one of the servants from the Grange whom he met when you met Miss Lindon?"

"Possible," Hunter said doubtfully.

"Not really," Lindon disputed. "You might not be an exacting master, but my wife is most assuredly an exacting mistress. She only travelled with one maid, who would not have dared dally with anyone, handsome valet or not. And I can't imagine your Orr making assignations with the coachman!"

"No, he preferred girls," Hunter said distractedly. "But that doesn't mean he didn't form a friendship with the coachman. Does he play cards?"

Lindon stared at him. "I have no idea."

"Just a thought," Hunter said apologetically. "Makes no difference really, because even if he did, why the devil would they go to Petteril's wood to play cards?"

"Gives them a reason to fall out, I suppose," Piers mused. "But no, there has to be a better reason for Orr to be there in the dark. Now that we know his name, I can ask my household if anyone knows him."

"Are *your* maids allowed assignations?" Hunter asked, still amused.

"I have no idea, but I suspect Mrs. Hicks rules them with a rod of iron."

"There's always ways to escape, though," April put in.

Hunter and Lindon regarded her in astonishment, as though one of the bricks had spoken.

"Risky," Piers said, and April nodded without lifting her eyes from the book where she was writing something.

Lindon poured them each another brandy. Hunter continued to watch April with some fascination.

"Just as a matter of interest," Piers said, "why did you leave the Dog and Duck so early in the morning?"

"I couldn't sleep, and I was in a hurry to see my friends," Lord Maxwell said carelessly, as though unaware of the implied insult to his current hosts for whom he did not trouble to wake early.

"Can we see his things?" Piers asked.

"Orr's?" Hunter dragged his attention back to him. "If you want to." He frowned. "I wonder what became of the bag he took with him?"

"And his boots," Piers said. "Or whatever footwear he had on. Maybe the bag was burned with his clothes."

"What a bizarre conversation," Hunter remarked.

"What sort of a man was he?" Piers drank his ale, regarding Hunter over the top.

Hunter shrugged. "Decent enough fellow. Decent enough valet. He didn't bother the maids, if that's what you mean. I don't keep maid-servants myself, but whenever we stay with other people, there's been no trouble."

"Where does he come from?" Piers asked. "Who is his family?"

Hunter shifted uncomfortably. "Can't remember, to be honest. If I ever knew. My man of business has a note of such things. I'll write to him today." He frowned. "I think he had a sister in Suffolk or Surrey. Or was it Sussex?"

"How long was he your valet?" Piers asked.

"A couple of years. Came recommended from Freddie Frobisher."

Lindon pounced this time. "Why did Frobisher let him go?"

"Pockets to let. Went abroad. There but for the grace of God go...
any of us." A hint of colour seeped into his cheeks, perhaps realizing
the tactlessness of such an observation to the man whose daughter was,
presumably, meant to extract him from similar difficulties.

"To your knowledge," Piers asked, "did he keep bad company ever?"

"Not that I know of. But then, I didn't really pay much attention,
as long as he did what I asked of him."

Lindon sighed. "A man doesn't, I suppose. Well, the inquest is tomorrow, but there's not really much doubt as to the verdict. Shall we
go? Put this out of our minds for a bit and do something more pleasant,
eh?"

The men stood and ambled off toward their respective carriages.

"Just a thought, Petteril," Hunter murmured, falling into step beside Piers. "But your girl there didn't have the assignation with Orr, did
she?

Piers regarded him. "He was dead before we came to Haybury. She
and I discovered the body on the day we arrived."

"Just wondered," Hunter said. "Taking little thing and seems
mighty interested in our conversation." He smiled slightly. "Don't look
like that. *I* don't bother other people's maids either."

Chapter Six

Lord Maxwell Hunter was not much given to deep thought. He preferred distraction, as a rule. But the murder of his servant was something that should concern even him and as he returned to Lindon Grange with his host, he couldn't help remembering the dead face, superimposed on the familiar but vital features he had seen so often. The conversation at the inn also stayed with him, echoing in loops.

Maxwell had always acknowledged his valet, treated him well and without the temper tantrums of some of his acquaintances. But he had never confided in the man. Nor had Orr ever talked about himself. Maxwell did not grieve for his servant, and he did not miss him except in a practical sense, but he was sorry the man was dead, and particularly in such a way.

And, if he was honest, the mystery of Orr's life now intrigued him more than it had when the man was alive. Petteril was responsible for that, of course, with his constant and unexpected questions. If Maxwell didn't know better, he could have imagined that Petteril actually cared.

Of course, Orr had been killed on Petteril's land, which probably focused the mind, but the depth of his interest was...unusual. But then, so was the man. Despite the rumours he had heard in London, Maxwell had expected someone eccentric and bookish and a little unworldly. Instead, the viscount appeared to have boundless energy of body and brain and was alarmingly up to snuff.

"Petteril's an odd fellow, is he not?" he said to Lindon as the carriage lumbered along the bumpy track to the Grange. "Charming, of course. But odd."

"Couldn't have put it better myself," Lindon said affably. "And I don't mind admitting, he has been very helpful over the murder of your poor man. Not used to such things here. Not used to them at all."

"Is Petteril?" Maxwell asked.

Lindon's eyebrows lifted in surprise. "I wouldn't have thought so. Clever fellow, though. Very clever."

"And curious," Maxwell said uneasily. "Too curious, I expect, in the circumstances."

Most people, after all, had things they would rather keep quiet—such as the fact that Maxwell had dashed off to Penny's house for a spot of pre-betrothal debauchery. Lindon wouldn't like that. Nor would Mrs. Lindon. God alone knew that the girl would think of it.

Intrigued by the thought, he found himself wondering for the first time what she was actually like. Beyond being a well brought up, biddable young lady with perfect manners and the ability to run a house. And a considerable fortune, of course, which would bail him out of his current difficulties, set them both up comfortably in his own little estate, and let them enjoy the Season in London if they chose.

Accordingly, in the hour before dinner, when he saw her from his bedchamber window, walking among the flowers in the garden below, he stopped to watch her. Just as he recalled from that distant party, she was pretty enough, and graceful enough to please a man's eye. Her evening gown was as lovely and as becoming as the pink morning gown she had worn earlier in the day. But her expression was over-serious, even troubled.

Did Orr's murder so close to her home bother her? Or was it something else? Trivial or important? In his experience, nothing very much at all went on in the heads of young society misses. Miss Lindon, of course, had no experience of the ton. She was the daughter of a country gentleman, a squire of no great distinction, however amiable and however much his wife might wish he was more. Maxwell knew he was marrying beneath him, but in the words of his father, who had reluctantly approved the match, "At least she's not some damned cit."

On impulse, he left his bedchamber, pausing only to drag the comb through his fashionable, short locks, and went in search of his betrothed.

He found her still in the garden, keeping to the paths so as not to dirty the hem of her gown. Was that a metaphor for her life? Did she ever stray from the path mapped out for her? Did she ever long to? The question produced an unexpected, unspecific longing in him. Was there really another path, another way, for anyone, least of all him?

But habit had taken over, and without any effort he contrived to bump into her at the end of the hedge bordering her current route. He was right. Beneath her modest gown were delightful, feminine curves. She gasped, jerking back from steadying arms.

"My lord! Forgive me, I was wool gathering and did not—"

"It was entirely my fault, ma'am," Maxwell interrupted with perfect truth. "I glimpsed you from the window and was rushing to find you."

"Why?" she asked warily.

Maxwell offered her his arm. "Don't you think it is a good idea to become a little better acquainted since we are to be married?"

"Are we?" she asked.

It was so unexpected that it felt like a bucketful of cold water landing on his head. Among the several emotions landing with it, he distinguished relief.

Perhaps she saw it. Certainly, the blush seeping along the line of her delicate cheekbones was interrupted by a fleeting smile.

"You have changed your mind?" he asked with at least outward calm. Time for another plan, perhaps.

Her eyes widened with deliberation. "From what?"

"From wishing to marry me."

"I have not been asked, sir," she said tartly.

He opened his mouth to retort, then, seeing the justice of her remark, inclined his head. "That is a fair point," he allowed. "An oversight that you probably find insulting, although it was never meant to be. Your father assured me you were willing to accept my offer."

"But you, my lord, are unwilling to make it."

She was right, of course. The loss of his freedom and at least some of his bachelor pleasures had certainly nagged at him, along with the annoying necessity of having to consider someone else. That was one reason he had bolted to Penny's on his way here. But God knew he wanted—needed—her money. And she had been a taking little thing at the Renforth's' party, a graceful dancing partner, her conversation fresh and unusually thoughtful, amusing... Or at least, she had laughed at his jokes. Young ladies were probably taught to do that along with how to be flatteringly attentive to a gentleman's every word.

Probably for the first time in his life, he felt gauche, and before he could remedy the matter, she changed the subject.

"Papa says the dead man in Petteril Wood is your valet."

With a further dose of confused relief and disappointment, he followed her lead. "Indeed. I am at a loss to know what the poor man was doing in the area as early as that. And why he would be in the wood in the middle of the night."

She turned her head, searching his face. He tried a smile, which generally had an effect on females.

Laura Lindon said, "You don't appear to be mourning him."

He blinked. "He was my servant. I'm sorry he is dead, of course."

"Of course." The smile flitting across her lips was neither happy nor quite amused. More...bitter. "The air has turned chilly. I shall go back to the house."

"Allow me to escort you."

"As you wish."

Even that sounded like a criticism, as though she knew he always did exactly as he wished and counted the cost later.

THE FOLLOWING MORNING, Piers rode out early with Sullivan Daniels, his steward, to learn something of his own land and the people who worked it. Everyone, from Daniels down, was curious about the corpse in Petteril Wood. Although the sheer quantity of repairs and improvements needing to be done was mind-boggling, he at least felt he was beginning to come to grips with the problems. He ordered the necessary repairs to tenants' houses and fences immediately and returned to the house in time for the staff reading lessons.

Again, April tidied up the table when the others had gone. "What d'you want me to do today?" she asked. "More room lists?"

"Later, if there's time," Piers said. "I want to find Orr's bag and boots and whatever means he used to travel from the Dog and Duck. And I want to know where Maxwell Hunter went when *he* left."

"You suspect him?" April said, with interest. "Surely he couldn't have done it if he didn't leave the Dog and Duck until after Orr."

"He could have left first—with Orr or following him—and come back during the night."

April scratched her cap and let her hand fall back in frustration. "Why would he do that? Why would he kill his own servant?"

"Temper? He admits to being annoyed enough with Orr to dismiss him. Men like Hunter often have no...boundaries to their behaviour. They feel entitled to exercise whatever impulses move them."

April looked doubtful. "Yes, but to stab a man to death just because he forgot to pack your bag before he took his leave..."

"It's a bit more terminal than turning him off without a character," Piers allowed. "But we only have his word as to the distant nature of their relationship. Gentlemen rely on their valets. It can be an oddly intimate relationship."

April's eyes widened. "You think they were...?"

"Not that kind of intimacy," Piers said hastily, appalled all over again by her awareness of life's frailties. "Or at least, not necessarily. He doesn't seem to approve of that kind of intimacy with servants. Though again, we only have his word. He was certainly looking at you."

Her mouth fell open, and then she laughed. "Nah. Only because I was a servant who spoke out of turn, and then he saw I was writing something."

"All the same, you will take care to avoid being alone with him. Or anyone else, come to that, until we discover who killed Orr. Go and get your cloak and..."

Mavis appeared in the doorway. "My lord, Mr. Alleyn has called to see you. He's waiting below."

"Oh, bring him up, then."

April made no effort to go, and he didn't dismiss her. She often had unexpected insight into people. In London she had noticed right away that Henry Devon was not to be trusted and seen, as Piers had not, that his cousin Gussie was afraid of her suitor.

"Alleyn's background is in trade," he murmured, "and his son is in love with Laura Lindon."

There was time for no more before quick footsteps in the passage heralded Mavis's announcement, "Mr. Alleyn, my lord."

Almost on her heels, a vigorous, greying man of middle years swept into the room like a whirlwind. His bow was more a forward jerk of the head, but he thrust out his hand with bluff friendliness, as though he were the host.

"Lord Petteril! Jeremiah Alleyn. Thought I'd come and introduce myself since we're neighbours."

"Delighted to meet you," Piers said, clasping his hand and having his own wrung to within an inch of actual pain.

Alleyn beamed. "Heard all about you from my Sally and my boy. And Lindon, of course. I hope you'll come and eat your mutton with us tonight. I've asked the Lindons and their distinguished guest, so you'll have plenty noble company, and my Sally does keep an excellent table."

In face of such enthusiastic friendliness, Piers would have found it difficult to refuse—as he suspected even Mrs. Lindon did—but in fact, he had no wish to. "Very kind of you. I should be delighted. In fact, I was going to call on you to talk about your land. My steward is impressed with your practises and wants to implement some of them here."

Alleyn looked suitably gratified. "Well, well, always happy to help. Not bred to the land like you fellows, but I'm all for progress and innovation! I won't keep you now. I suppose you'll be going to the inquest?"

"I'll need to, since I discovered the body."

Alleyn shook his head. "Terrible business. Shocking. Shocking. Until this evening, then!" He spun around and swept toward the door again. On the way, he caught sight of April for the first time, peered at her, and nodded without slowing down. The door seemed to close itself behind him, as if he had willed it with the sheer force of his personality, leaving Piers blinking.

April grinned. "I like him."

APRIL'S DISTRUST OF the empty, open spaces of the countryside began to disintegrate that morning, largely because Lord Petteril let her hold the reins and drive the horses. He gave her gloves and showed her how to hold the reins, his touch cool and impersonal, then sat back and watched for the most part, occasionally issuing casual instructions. She walked them, then trotted them, and then, on Petteril's say-so, encouraged them into a canter. From sheer delight, she spared an instant to grin at him. She had a glimpse of his watchful face, a proud smile playing on his lips.

No one had ever been proud of April. She'd never been a very good thief. Before Lord Petteril, people had tended to knock her out of the way in irritation. He praised her reading, her thinking, and now her driving. Which, stupidly, made her want to preen. It wasn't praise that made her stay, though. She had always known that.

"Pull up here," he said. They were a hundred yards or so beyond where they had stopped before. "Draw gently on the reins and tell them to *Woah.*"

Enchanted by the horses' obedience, she managed to slow them and finally bring them to a halt.

"Good," he said, taking the reins from her to let her alight. "You have a light touch. Always best."

April jumped down. He tossed her the reins and she looped them around a suitable tree branch.

After that they spent a frustrating couple of hours searching the road and the woods near where they had found the body, moving toward the Dog and Duck and the town of Blanchester where the inquest was to be held. They found normal traces of horses and vehicles on the road, which was only to be expected, but very little of interest in the wood itself. Although they discovered very faint hoofprints on one of the forest tracks, some distance from the clearing, it was impossible to tell how old they were.

"They do seem to go in both directions, though," Lord Petteril remarked. "Both to and from the road."

April, who still didn't quite trust the close, eerie quiet of the forest, glanced uneasily over her shoulder. She kept hearing movement in the undergrowth, scurrying and sudden cracks and rustlings, as though someone was watching them, observing them. The hairs on the back of her neck stood up, but since Lord Petteril didn't seem to notice, she preferred not to appear scared. Instead, she dragged her attention back to what he had just said.

"As if Orr rode here, left his horse and walked to the clearing," she mused. "And then, what? His killer prigged his horse and rode home again?"

"It's possible," Lord Petteril said. "But nothing to prove it. Why here, of all places?"

"Because they knew Haybury Court was empty, with not enough outside servants to keep the grounds clear of poachers? Orr prob'ly wouldn't have known that, but his killer might."

"And arranged their meeting here to—er... croak him. Again, possible. But why? How annoying can a valet *be* to anyone not his master? Unless he had connections to the criminal world we know nothing of yet. Or..." He paused, gazing into the trees, while she fidgeted.

"What?" April demanded after several seconds of silence. "Do you think someone else is nearby?"

His eyes refocused on her. "Too soft. Probably just animals."

"Then what you looking at?"

"I was just thinking. Perhaps Orr was killed in mistake for his master."

"There'll be lots of reasons to kill *him*," April said with enthusiasm as they walked back toward where they had left the curricle. "All we said before when we thought it *was* him who was dead. That cove who's in love with Miss Lindon for one. Or perhaps her brother disapproves of him, followed Laura to an assignation she'd made with Maxwell and did him in for honour's sake."

Lord Petteril glanced at her. "Have you been reading lurid romance novels?"

"No, but I'd like to. Have you got any? For practise, like?"

He grinned openly, which always made her smile back, even though his smiles were no longer quite so rare. "Maybe. I'll look. Come on, we'd better bustle about or we'll be late for the inquest."

"Or dinner," April said hopefully.

"You can never have too many dinners."

"Then maybe I could have one while you're in the court," April suggested. The law made her uneasy.

"There is no court. The hearing will be in the inn, and it's only to establish the official cause of death."

"Any idiot could see that," April said scornfully. "He had a bloody great knife in his heart."

"Well, the doctor might have something more interesting to report," Lord Petteril said, although she could see he doubted it.

By the time they arrived, the inn was already full of important men, gathered at one end of the room. April was foiled in her intention to slink quietly away by the simple fact there was nowhere to slink to. Even most of the chairs were being taken by respectable men who were apparently the jury, now seating themselves to one side of the tables before Mr. Lindon, the gentleman who was coroner, according to Piers, and the man busy taking notes.

"They've just been to view the body," Piers murmured. He made some signal to the innkeeper, pointing to April, and she realized that he was ordering her a meal.

In return, she said, "Dr. Rose is sitting facing the beaks. With Lord Maxwell Hunter. And the younger Alleyn is sitting behind them."

Petteril's eyebrows flew up. "Samuel Alleyn? I wonder what brings him here?" He made his way across to sit by Alleyn, leaving her to sit alone in the quiet corner and eat her dinner.

Apart from holding them in the public inn, the proceedings were very formal and dull. The coroner cove droned on for a bit about the jury's duty, having seen the body. April, beginning to feel safe, tucked into her mutton stew, while Lord Maxwell stood up and confirmed Orr's name and employment with himself.

Only when Lord Petteril was called to stand and give evidence of where and when he had discovered the body, did April's alarm return with a vengeance. Would they ask her, too?

But his lordship's statement was brief and succinct and made no mention of her at all. There was obviously no reason to doubt his word, and after saying he informed the magistrate by letter of his discovery, he sat down.

As the coroner moved on to Dr. Rose, April breathed again and returned to her mutton.

Having explained how Mr. Lindon had sent him to the Red Lion, where the constables had taken the body, he proceeded to the cause of death, the clear wound to the heart by the hunting knife, also viewed by the coroner and jury.

The coroner leaned forward and addressed the doctor. "In your opinion, could this injury had been self-inflicted?"

"No," said Dr. Rose, much more firmly than in the Red Lion cellar.

"On what grounds?"

"Partly because the angle of the wound makes it unlikely. Mostly because when I examined the wound more closely, I found threads in it."

"Threads?" the coroner repeated in surprise.

"From his clothing, sir. The knife thrust them deep into the wound. And his clothing, as you have already heard, was burned. I have matched the threads with some of the scorched rags that remain. Therefore, it is my judgement that he must have been killed with his clothes on, and that someone, presumably the murderer, then removed his clothes and burned them."

"GOOD WORK," PIERS MURMURED to Rose when the doctor had sat back down.

"I thought so," Dr. Rose said, with the flicker of a smile.

Inevitably the jury brought in the verdict of murder by person or persons unknown, and Dr. Rose thanked and dismissed them. By then, Piers already felt the movement beside him, and saw Samuel Alleyn striding toward the door. He was the only one of the neighbours who had attended, except for those obliged to.

Piers filed out with Hunter and Dr. Rose. At the corner table, April was finishing the last mouthful of her meal. Seeing him leave, she took an unladylike slurp of beer and stood up. She raised her hand, clearly about to wipe her mouth on her sleeve, then caught his eye and lowered it again, to drag a somewhat grubby handkerchief from her bag instead.

Piers's lips twitched, but he pretended not to notice.

"Sympathies on your loss, Lord Maxwell," Dr. Rose said. "Afraid I have an appointment and must run. Lord Petteril." He bowed and strode off.

There was no sign of Samuel Alleyn. Clearly not in a talkative mood.

"Now it's over to me," Lindon said gloomily, coming out to join Hunter and Petteril. "Dashed if I know how to find the poor man's killer. He'll be miles away by now."

"Maybe not," Petteril said. "Find anything interesting among his things that Hunter brought?"

"No, nor anywhere else." Lindon sighed. "Come back to the Grange, if you like, and look for yourself. But as Hunter said, there's no sign of hair brushes or shaving kit, toothpowder—the things one would need overnight. Or the small bag Maxwell remembers him carrying with the larger when they travel."

"Perhaps he didn't plan to go back to the Dog and Duck that same night," Piers said thoughtfully. "Or, probably, associate with the disreputable, who would not care about a shadowed chin and uncombed hair."

"Perhaps he really did have an assignation," Hunter said in apparent surprise. "Though I can't imagine who with."

"Not much of a ladies' man?" Piers hazarded.

"No idea, to be honest. Beyond the fact he kept the line with other people's staff."

April was walking around the side of the inn to fetch the curricle.

Piers made a decision. "Tell you what, I'll drop over tomorrow to see his things. I need to go home and change before dinner at the Alleyns. I understand you're going, too?"

Lindon wrinkled his nose. "Difficult to say no."

"Affable fellow," Maxwell observed. "Though his son isn't so friendly."

"He's not so thick-skinned," Piers said. "They all know they're looked down on by those of us with longer blood lines and less wealth, but he feels it."

Lindon looked baffled, but to his credit, Hunter appeared to consider the possibility. Piers stepped back and made his farewells, then went to meet April who was leading the horses toward him.

"Can I drive again?" she asked hopefully.

"Not this time. We're in a hurry. I want to call in at the Dog and Duck before we go home."

He set off, saluting with his whip to Lindon and Maxwell, who were about to climb into Lindon's coach. Maxwell stood back to examine the Petteril equipage as the horses trotted smartly past.

They left the town at a spanking pace, and rolled up to the Dog and Duck, just outside the town, at half past three o'clock. Adopting his imperious viscount role for the occasion, Piers left April with the horses and stalked into the inn, where he requested the presence of the landlord in tones that brooked no delay.

The innkeeper, one Bolton, was duly obsequious, even when informed he would not, that day, have the pleasure of serving his lordship with more than information. His lordship condescended to a small brandy.

"So tell me, when exactly did Nathaniel Orr, Lord Maxwell Hunter's valet, leave the premises on Monday?"

"Around five o'clock in the afternoon. I remember 'cause it's a busy time for us and he appeared in the taproom without warning, wanting to hire a horse."

Piers blinked. "Did he, by God? Was Lord Maxwell with him?"

"No, no, his lordship had given him a couple of days' leave. Or so Mr. Orr said."

"So you rented a horse to Orr. What did he have with him?"

Bolton scratched his ear in thought. "Small carpet bag," he said triumphantly. "Strapped it to the saddle and off he went."

"Did he say where? Or when he'd be back?"

"He said *tomorrow*, as I recall. He said as he's to pack his lordship's bags for him early, like."

And yet Orr had taken an overnight bag. "And did Orr come back?"

"No."

"Didn't that bother you?"

"Only that his lordship seemed in a grump that his bags hadn't been packed. He didn't threaten me, mind, but I wouldn't have liked to have been in Orr's shoes." He broke off, colour flooding his already florid face. "Not that I'm accusing Lord Maxwell of nothing! His mind was on dismissal, not violence."

"And Lord Maxwell left in his own vehicle on Tuesday morning?"

"Yes, like I told the constables Mr. Lindon sent."

Piers regarded him fixedly. There was something of the rehearsed speech in much of what Bolton was saying. Piers had taken that as inevitable since he must already have told the constables the same things. But he hadn't told the constables everything, and there was a faintly uneasy look in his eye.

Piers said, "You didn't tell the constables about Orr going off in the middle of the night and not coming back."

"They only asked about gentlemen!" Bolton said indignantly. "And his lordship said openly he was going to Lindon Grange. The valet didn't say where he was going."

"Weren't you even bothered about the horse not coming back?"

Bolton's face cleared. "Oh, he came back, my lord. Barnes, over at the Red Lion sent him back Tuesday evening."

Piers didn't know whether to be annoyed or amused. The wretched animal had been at Red Lion when he went there to see what the doctor had discovered. Abandoned in the wood, it must have found its own way to a stable it knew.

"Apparently the horse was found still with its saddle on at Barnes's stable, as though it had wandered in itself. Barnes thought as someone had been avoiding paying."

Piers sighed. There was no point in being angry with the innkeeper. The constables just hadn't asked the right questions of the right people, and he couldn't really expect Bolton to know what was important.

"Would you know," he asked, wandering over to the front door, "if anyone had left the inn during the night?"

"I bolted the doors at eleven, and they were still bolted at six when I came down on Tuesday morning."

More virtuous recitation. Piers looked at the stout front door. There were three bolts and one large key lock.

"Did you turn the lock, too?"

"Don't usually," Bolton admitted. "No point, unless we're all out at once, and we never are, not when we've customers."

Then Hunter could easily have left during the night and caught up with Orr, either by accident or because he knew where the valet was going. And he could have made it to Petteril Wood and back to the Dog and Duck before six when the innkeeper got up.

"Did Lord Maxwell bring a riding horse with him as well as his carriage cattle?"

"Yes, he did. Expect you'll find it over at Lindon Grange."

"Expect I will. I don't suppose you noticed if this riding horse was tired in the morning?"

Bolton began to look harassed. "Can't say as I did. It went off with the rest, tied behind the carriage. Will that be all, my lord."

Piers remembered to look haughty. "No. Did he pay his shot before he left or leave his direction for your bill?"

Bolton hesitated. "He left his direction."

Because he had left before the inn was stirring, Piers suspected and had somehow charmed his host into silence. Well, Piers didn't want to drive the man into a corner either. "I don't suppose you kept that direction?"

Bolton, apparently pleased to be able to help again, delved beneath the counter and came up with a grubby note bearing Lord Maxwell's name and direction beyond Trowbridge, care of one Mr. Gabriel Pennyfeather.

"Bit of a bachelor party?" Piers hazarded.

Bolton blushed. "Think so, my lord."

"Did you get paid?"

"Money came back by return."

So he really had been at Pennyfeather's, without much time to stop off in Petteril Wood to murder his valet. Unless he had left the Dog and Duck early in the night.

Piers said, "Had Lord Maxwell's bed been slept in on Monday night?"

"'Course it had!"

"I believe," Piers said, "I should speak to your chamber maid."

But the girl, duly summoned, maintained she would have noticed if the bed had *not* been slept in. She changed the sheets after Lord Maxwell's departure.

"He could just have rumpled up the sheets to fool her," April pointed out when he gave her the jist of what he had learned.

"He could have. Or he could have come back and slept for an hour or two before setting off from the inn." Piers sighed. "Things is, I can't see him behaving that way. Too much effort to kill a valet he could simply push out of a window, and absolutely no motive."

"Unless Orr was running away from him. Maybe he was a cruel master or expected unnatural favours."

Piers stared at her. "Apart from the knife wound, Orr's body was unmarked. No signs of cruelty. As for the favours... I wish you hadn't said that."

"Ain't a pleasant thing to do to someone who can't say no," April said austerely. "Male or female."

"I know. Maxwell just doesn't strike me as that sort of predator. And he's too damned aware of females." He sighed. "But we still can't rule him out."

Chapter Seven

Samuel Alleyn had given himself very little time to change for dinner.

"Sam!" his mother exclaimed, coming out into the hall as soon as she heard his tread on the tiled floor. She was already dressed for the evening, her silk gown too fussy for her short, plump figure, her jewels too many and too...obvious. "Where have you been?"

"I went to the inquest," he replied, heading for the stairs.

If his mother was surprised, she hid it. "Well, hurry, for goodness sake, our guests will be here any minute!"

She did not ask about the inquest, for which he was glad. He was not even sure why he had attended. Partly, he had hoped to discover some weakness or even silliness in his rival for Laura Lindon's love. Some hope, he thought savagely, hurling his clothes at the floor before splashing water over his hands and face and neck. The man had stood with perfect poise and given his brief evidence matter-of-factly and without fuss. Clearly, it had never entered his head that anyone could suspect him of any crime, let alone of murdering his servant.

They wouldn't hang a marquis's son, he reflected with regret, dressing quickly and efficiently without the aid of a valet. But surely, guilt would force him to flee the country and Laura could never marry such a man. Which would leave the field open for Samuel.

He donned his coat, shook out his cuffs and turned to the glass, dragging his mind from Lord Maxwell to himself.

Who are trying to fool? he asked his reflection and curled his lip. He looked the perfect gentleman, dressed for dinner in dark attire with a jet and diamond pin in his elegantly tied cravat, sleeve buttons to match. He stood straight, if not as tall as Lord Maxwell Bloody Hunter, and he was not bad looking. His eyes were clearer, his face unmarked by the lines of dissipation already marring Hunter's, though his lordship could not have been more than two or three years older. But Samuel was no rival of the aristocrat's son.

Samuel had been educated as a gentleman, always well aware that no one who truly mattered would ever see him as such. He was merely Alleyn the mill owner's son, who took a bit of an eccentric interest in agriculture, even though he was never born to the land. His father had bought it with money earned in trade.

Once, he had foolishly imagined his birth would not matter to Laura Lindon, that she would be able to talk her father round. After all, she had always been kind to him, friendly enough to give him hope—before the bombshell news that she was betrothed.

Only then, he recalled, dragging his heels on his way downstairs, had he truly realized how much his emotions had been engaged. At first, he had merely wanted to be accepted, and marriage to Laura, with the Lindons on his side, would have ensured that, at least locally. But once his hope was taken away, he realized how much he had grown to love her. And it was unbearable.

His mother, already in the drawing room with his father, beamed at him. "How smart and handsome you look! Doesn't he, Jeremiah?"

"Aye, he does that. Cleverest in the neighbourhood, too."

Samuel gritted his teeth. He valued his parents, and they could not help their vulgarity. They had not had his education.

"I have a dozen things to do before morning," he fumed. "Why on earth did you invite them all, Mama?"

Her eyebrows flew up in surprise. "For you, of course, dear. It's good to have friends your own age."

He bit back the response that most if not all their guests would laugh themselves silly at the prospect of being friends with Samuel Alleyn the mill owner's son. Which was fortunate because at that moment, the vicar and his wife were announced, and the excruciating evening began.

The vicar's wife was a good-natured, ineffectual lady, permanently worried, no doubt in case someone would forget her husband's vocation and verbally annihilate the prosy old bore. Fortunately, before the vicar grew too sententious, the Lindons arrived in a flurry of condescension and arrogance.

Lindon himself was bearable, Samuel allowed, shaking the squire's hand in welcome, if not overburdened with intelligence. He was wealthy for a mere country squire—or at least he always appeared so, though his land could earn better for him—but he seemed to have few ambitions beyond doing what his ancestors had always done.

No, his wife, Evangela, was the ambitious one. Samuel bowed punctiliously over her hand, which she withdrew almost as soon as he touched it. In her youth, Evangela had enjoyed a London Season and wanted the same for her daughter who was easily pretty enough to make a grand match with the aristocracy. In the end, of course, it hadn't taken a London Season, only another country party and an encounter with the man facing him now.

Lord Maxwell Hunter was everything Samuel was not, with all the enviable poise and confidence that comes from birth. The world did not see a foolish young man who squandered his privilege in vice. Like the Lindons, everyone saw a charming man of fashion, a bit of a rakehell, perhaps, but young gentlemen must sow their wild oats. And then marry money.

Laura was his money, and that injustice boiled Samuel's blood. It was an effort to shake the man's hand, but Hunter had offered and he could not be so churlish—or so gauche —as to refuse it. Oddly, there was no distaste or condescension in Lord Maxwell's attitude, just a glimmer of surprise, as though he had actually sensed Samuel's hostility.

Refusing to back down, Samuel held the gaze and forced a smile while he wished the man at Jericho, or anywhere, really, that he could not take Laura. It was Hunter who moved aside, making way for Oscar Lindon to join them.

Oscar's superior nod always felt like he was acknowledging a servant who was trying hard. Which was probably how he saw Samuel. Once, it had annoyed him. Now, Oscar's contempt bothered him least of all because Laura had always opposed it.

Laura.

She smiled at him, warming and breaking his heart. "Good evening, Sam. What are you scowling about? Have I a smut on my nose?"

He blushed at her teasing, and at her use of his name. "Of course not. I suppose I am thinking about the tragedy in Petteril Wood, although it is hardly a fit subject for a dinner party."

"No, it isn't," Oscar said flatly, glaring at him. Then he turned, looking around the gathered guests, all now with a glass of sherry or ratafia. "But talking of Petteril, where is he?"

PETTERIL, IN FACT, was at the foot of the Alleyn's gardens, using a forked stick to poke a boot out of the gardener's fire.

It was the smell that had drawn him as the smoke drifted in through the carriage window. April's words about the scent of plague had come back to him. Because among the wood smoke he could smell something else, neither food nor wool...

On impulse, he had knocked on the carriage roof to make Mickey the coachman pull up, but he was on the ground even before the horses were still, following his nose through the elm trees to the gardener's fire.

It looked almost like an oven—a stone enclosure with a large gap at the front and a chimney to carry the smoke above head hight. A young gardener came out of the nearby wooden hut as Piers strode up to the

fire and crouched down beside the heap of garden rubbish waiting to
go on. Piers peered through the gap and excitement soared.

Reaching blindly he found a stick and used to draw out the object
he had seen—scorched and charred around the edges but not yet properly burned, it landed between Piers and the gardener. A black leather
boot.

Even better, disturbing the fire had revealed traces of its partner. He
poked that out too, causing the gardener to step smartly out of the way
and scattering ash all over the place.

"Sir!" the gardener protested.

Piers stood up, brushing off his clothes and gazing with satisfaction
at the smouldering remains. Slowly, he raised his eyes to the youth's annoyed face. "Why are you burning boots?"

"I'm not!"

Piers pointed to the salvage between them. One was definitely
boot-shaped. The other clearly had been not so long ago.

"Well I didn't put 'em there," the gardener said, scratching his head.
"What'd I burn good boots for? Or worn ones, come to that. Someone
else must have dropped 'em in."

"But burning the rubbish is your job."

"Dead leaves and pruned wood," the boy said, beginning to panic.
"Not kitchen stuff and certainly not house stuff. Whose boots are
they?"

"I'm not sure yet. When did you light the fire?"

"Just ten minutes ago, but I built it up last evening. Too late to burn
it then so I waited."

"Would any of the other gardeners have added things to it during
the day?"

"No, they leave stuff on the heap here. It's my job to look after burning it. I'm good at it."

"I can see that you are," Piers soothed.

"I didn't put no boots in there." The lad sounded earnest and not a little alarmed, so Piers smiled at him.

"No, someone else clearly did that. Not your fault." He took out his handkerchief and gingerly picked up the pieces of boot. They weren't smoking anymore, but he could still feel the heat through his gloves.

The gardener stared after him, his mouth open. Which was nothing to the expression of the Alleyns' butler when he appeared at the front door with the leather remains in one hand and smelling vaguely of smoke.

"Petteril," Piers said amiably. "I believe Mrs. Alleyn is expecting me."

"Of course, my lord," the butler said, his gaze fixed on the boots as he ushered Piers inside.

Piers gave him his hat and placed the boots on the floor while he removed his gloves and coat and handed them to the waiting footman. He pointed at the charred footwear. "Don't move those, yet, if you please. I'll explain to Mr. and Mrs. Alleyn."

The butler, who had no doubt heard of the many eccentricities attributed to him, forbore to comment and led him to the drawing room, where Mrs. Alleyn welcomed him with apparent happiness, not unmixed with relief.

"Why there you are, my lord! We were just wondering about your safety. Especially with what happened in your wood."

Piers bowed over her hand. "Apologies for causing undue concern. Very happy to meet you again, Mrs. Alleyn."

"Glass of sherry, my lord?" Alleyn offered.

Piers shook hands with him, too, then smiled and bowed to the company in general. "Hunter," he said, picking out Lord Maxwell more by his rakish stance than anything else. "Might I borrow you for just a moment? One minute, Mrs. Alleyn, I assure you."

Hunter looked startled and then amused as he murmured, "Excuse me," to his hostess, and followed Piers from the room.

Piers strode back across the hall, Hunter prowling after him in hope, it seemed, of further amusement. Piers pointed at the sorry-looking boots in pride of place before the coat stand.

Hunter gazed from them to Piers, his eyes gleaming. "I use Hoby myself, if you're looking for recommendation. But my dear fellow, what did you do to them? Run all the way back from Blanchester?"

"Oh, they're not mine. I was hoping you might recognize them."

"Not mine either, old fellow. And forgive me for saying so, but they stink."

"Yes, I pulled them out of a fire."

"Beyond use, sadly."

Piers picked up the almost-whole, charred boot and set it, tattered soul downward, beside Hunter's gleaming shoe, then looked up, meeting Hunter's puzzled, not entirely serious gaze.

"How big," he asked, straightening, "were Nathaniel Orr's feet, compared to yours?"

The mirth vanished from Lord Maxwell's face. His mouth tightened. "You think they're Orr's boots?"

"We never found them. Somebody stuck these in with the garden rubbish for burning."

There was a hint of distaste but no fear in Hunter's face as he bent and picked up the boot. "They could be Orr's," he said reluctantly. "He was around the same height and build as me and I don't recall his feet being out of proportion." He handed the boot to Piers. "I can't swear that they're his. I never paid much attention to what he wore. It was fitting and smart and I saw no more than that."

"Well, he looked after your dress, not you his," Piers said excusingly. After all, he could not have described Stewart's footwear from an hour ago when the man had helped him dress for dinner.

He stooped and picked up the other bit of boot and looked around for a footman, into whose surprised hands he deposited all the remains.

"Could you make this into a parcel for Mr. Lindon? I'll explain it to him."

OSCAR LINDON WATCHED the two aristocrats return to Mrs. Alleyn's drawing room, both expensively dressed in similar fashion, apart from the two quizzing glasses on black ribbon hung around Petteril's neck, and yet each owing their distinction to something else entirely.

Hunter was a rakehell, of course, a devil with the ladies, and an expensive wastrel, but a good-natured one. Oscar would hardly have promoted his sister's marriage to a truly Bad Man. Hunter would waste her fortune if he could, but on Oscar's advice, the solicitors had so hemmed in the settlements that Hunter would only get his hands on so much of it. The important thing about Lord Maxwell was his father and brother, both political giants, and as family, able to introduce Oscar into the first circles of society.

Oscar had political aspirations himself. And he fully intended to marry into the top drawer, too. When the time was right. Oh yes, Hunter was a good ally.

Petteril... Oddly, he had never considered Piers until now when he stood beside Lord Maxwell, and actually compared favourably—an opinion that startled Oscar who remembered him largely as the runt of a rumbunctious litter, despised as the youngest and later bullied for being different. Oscar had never truly despised his scholarship, but he hadn't expected the diffident boy to turn into this confidently eccentric man who somehow dominated the room. How had that happened? Petteril was a clever man and people would listen to him...

His stomach dived.

Had be backed the wrong horse? Would Petteril not make a better brother-in-law? *He* would not waste Laura's fortune; and he had a seat in the House of Lords which Hunter did not. Not that Petteril seemed politically inclined, but still, he could be encouraged, influenced, manipulated...

Was it too late to change horses? Laura would be mortified, even if she didn't appear to care much for Lord Maxwell. But Hunter's reputation was an excellent excuse to jilt him.

No rushing. He should take some time to reacquaint himself with this new version of Piers Withan. He took the opportunity as they walked into dinner in a huddle—the numbers were too uneven to trouble with formal partners and he doubted such etiquette troubled the Alleyns in any case.

"I suppose you were at the inquest?" he said casually to Petteril, catching up with him in the hall. "No surprises, according to my father."

"Not really," Petteril agreed.

"My father thinks the culprit is probably this highwayman. He held Alleyn up, you know. And someone told Papa this afternoon that he's still lurking around Blanchester."

Petteril's straight eyebrows flew upward. "Really? Why? Are there such rich pickings around here that he risks capture and hanging?"

"I wouldn't have thought so. Rumour says he's injured or ill, though. After all, old Alleyn did manage to shoot him."

Petteril looked thoughtful but said only, "We think we've found his boots."

"The highwayman's?" Oscar said, startled.

"Orr's. The dead man's."

Oscar flushed. "Does it prove anything?"

"It certainly indicates that whoever killed Orr passed by this house at some point between yesterday evening and this."

Oscar stopped dead, staring at him. As Samuel brushed past them, he lowered his voice. "Never tell me you suspect Alleyn? Or Samuel? Good God!"

"Why would either of them do such a thing?" Petteril wondered innocently. His gaze, however, was *not* innocent. Oscar had never seen such clear, penetrating eyes. Had they always been like that and he had never noticed? Because he was so taken with the older, more likely heirs.

"I can't imagine," Oscar said. "You must be wrong."

"I could be." A dazzling smile flickered across his face and vanished. "Actually, I was wondering if your highwayman passed this way and stuffed the boots into the Alleyns' fire *en route*, as it were."

"Well, the constables are looking for him," Oscar said, without much hope of their ever finding him.

AFTER HER MEAL WITH the Haybury Court servants, it was too dark for April to examine any more rooms in the house. It seemed natural to help the others clear up and make things ready for the morning, both in the servants' hall and in the main house. Mrs. Hicks appeared amazed to see her doing anything so menial as washing dishes, or carrying a coal scuttle, or helping set the table in the breakfast parlour.

"Does his lordship expect you to be doing this?" she asked, catching April crossing the hall with a fresh pile of starched linen napkins for the breakfast table.

"I don't know," April admitted. "I like to be busy." Which was true. Now she no longer had to plot and fight for every scrap of food, she found too much time to herself weighed heavily on her.

Mrs. Hicks pulled her brow down into a frown, gazing fixedly at April, who, with difficulty, did her the courtesy of standing still. "What's he got you looking all over the house for? What are you writing down?"

"Just what needs freshening up and what colours would suit it. I like colours and I saw what he liked from what he ordered in the London house."

Mrs. Hicks stared some more, seemed about to say something, then walked away, saying over her shoulder. "Get on with those napkins, then."

As she joined the other servants in the hall for a last mouthful before bed, she sensed a very faint softening toward her. Which could offer a little more pleasantness to life in the country.

Nevertheless, before the doors were locked, she found herself slipping away to see Benson and the horses in the stables. She missed Benson's calm company.

Jem now blushed whenever she came by and barely dared speak to her. But Carter, the head groom, unbent somewhat and she spent some time listening to all the horse talk and asking questions while she sneaked a few treats to the horses, purloined from the kitchen.

She was still there when the sounds of Lord Petteril's return had Jem bolting around to the front of the house to meet the horses. She was even helping to brush down one of the carriage horses when the Professor's stamp and whinny told her Petteril himself approached.

His cravat loosened and his coat buttons open, he strolled into the lantern light, casually greeting the grooms and asking after all the horses as he inspected them and petted each.

"I think Orion's doing better already, don't you?" he said.

"He is that, my lord," Carter replied. "Needed the exercise. These old fellows seem perkier, too." He referred to the carriage horses, one of which April was currently brushing.

Lord Petteril blinked at her.

She said defiantly. "I was just here when Jem brought them in."

"And you like horses," he said mildly. "I know." He patted the horse on the other side of his neck. "But the house doors are all locked. You'll have to come back in the front with me."

Benson took the brush from her.

As they walked around the house, April sped up to walk alongside him rather than behind. "What'd you learn at the Alleyns' dinner?" she demanded.

She could hear the smile in his voice as he answered. "I found Orr's boots. Or at least Hunter said they *could* be Orr's boots. They're the right sort of size."

"Cor! Where were they?"

"In the garden fire at Alleyn's."

She stopped dead, then had to run to catch him up again. "You think Samuel did it? Mistaking Orr for Maxwell?"

"It's possible. Samuel had never met either of them before, to my knowledge. He surely wants Maxwell out of the way, and he was interested enough to attend the inquest."

"Guilty conscience?" April suggested. "Or was he hoping to catch Maxwell out in some lie to prove *he* done it?"

"Either is possible. I just can't imagine how he would have lured the wrong man to Petteril Wood. And if they met there by accident, what the devil was either of them doing there?"

"I suppose the same would go for old Mr. Alleyn," April said, deflated.

"And Mrs. Alleyn. But if they picked their time, anyone could have stashed the boots into the fire among the garden rubbish. It was laid last night. It doesn't need to have been any of the household."

April grimaced with disgust. "You mean someone meant to throw suspicion on the Alleyns, deliberately? That's mean."

"Vindictive," Lord Petteril agreed. "In which case, the boots don't even have to be Orr's, or the person who placed them the murderer. Unlikely, I agree, but the local gentry would certainly prefer someone more refined at Barnwood."

"You mean the Lindons would," April said bluntly.

"And the vicar. He seems to see the devil in trade."

"That's daft."

"Unless Alleyn's trading from the temple, yes," Petteril said obscurely.

April frowned. "What temple?"

His face turned toward her, the lantern at his side casting flickering light over his lean, clever face. "You should go to church on Sunday."

"Why?"

"Then you'd learn stories from the Bible, like Christ throwing the traders out of the temple."

"Why'd he do that?"

"Because the temple was for worshiping God. Like the church."

"I don't believe in God," April blurted. "Or if I do, I don't like him. It ain't just the bad people who suffer. In fact, it's the other way round. And your vicar don't sound very nice either."

She met his gaze defiantly, expecting shock or even anger, but not the flash of pity and something very like guilt that she glimpsed before he turned his eyes back to the path and veered right toward the front door.

"He isn't very nice," Lord Petteril agreed. "But I doubt he murdered anyone, let alone tried to blame it on Alleyn. It doesn't have to have been a deliberate attempt to incriminate. It could have been opportunistic."

"The murderer happened across the fire by chance?" She had to guess his meaning and was stupidly proud to see him nod in reply. "What, and they just happened to be carrying the boots?"

"Maybe. The killer might just have been looking for a place to hide them so he weren't discovered with them. Especially if he was this highwayman—who is rumoured to be still in the area, incidentally. Alleyn was telling us about his adventure with him last market day. He thinks it was the infamous Brandy Bill, so called because he is meant to have added insult to injury by once toping his victim's brandy."

"What, they think he's still in Blanchester? Don't make sense, mister. Besides, a highwayman wouldn't have burned clothes *or* boots."

"I've been thinking about that. He might have if he was ill or injured and wanted to avoid a hue and cry. He might have panicked seeing his victim looked like a gentleman."

"Why'd he kill him in the first place, then?"

"Robbery. In the dark, he might not have seen Orr's clothes until the deed was done."

April considered. She knew well enough that life was cheap to those with nothing. And those who took to the high toby would be hanged if caught. Adding murder to the charges made no difference to that. Though killing a nob was liable to bring down much more attention that was sensible.

"Possible," she said reluctantly. "Where is this scamp man then?"

"Lindon thinks he's hiding somewhere in Blanchester." Lord Petteril put his key in the door and opened it. He glanced down at April. "How would I go about finding him?"

"Don't ask," she said, alarmed.

"I am asking."

"I mean don't ask in Blanchester," she said. "I know you found me that way in St, Giles. And you asked about Lord, too, though you shouldn't have 'cause it'd have got you killed pretty soon if you'd hung around. This high toby cove ain't me—he's got a lot more to lose and if he's hidden, he's got other nasty coves looking out for him."

Even as she warned him off, the thought was already in her mind. *I could find him. Ape could find him no bother.*

Chapter Eight

April's plans were thwarted the following morning by Mavis the maid spilling scalding hot tea over her hand. Mrs. Hicks was furious, because she was interviewing prospective footmen at the time, and besides, Lord Petteril had just told her Mrs. Lindon was planning to call on the morrow, bringing her own guests, and there was a mountain of work to be done.

"We don't know what to do with guests," Mavis confided to April, nursing her painful and well-bandaged hand. "And Mrs. Hicks barely remembers. I couldn't have picked a worse time to do something so stupid."

"Anyone can have an accident," April said. "I have 'em all the time. I'll muck in to help, but I ain't trained to it like you."

"You're a funny sort of a maid," Mavis reflected, though not with any malice.

And in fact, April was only too aware that she wasn't a maid at all, not in the ways that mattered to Mavis or Mrs. Hicks. What she found she was good at, was organizing.

She had the gardener's boy cut the lawn, just in case the weather was pleasant tomorrow, and Carter reckoned it would be. Apparently, his injured leg confided such secrets. She had tables and chairs hauled out of unused rooms and helped clean them to a shine, while Mrs. Hicks dealt with what she knew—directing the maids to clean the dining room, the salons leading onto the terrace and the lawn, and the drawing room just in case the weather was not as fine as Carter foretold. The two footman, duly chosen that morning, were set to work in the afternoon, cleaning the windows outside and in, and climbing up ladders to clean all the high places a long-handled broom or mop couldn't reach.

Lord Petteril himself was out most of the day with Mr. Daniels the steward, so April could not consult him about her ideas, she simply did them or suggested they be done and, remarkably, they usually were. At some point, while poking about in the wine cellar, she realized she was enjoying herself.

LAURA LINDON WAS SECRETLY amused when, over breakfast, Lord Maxwell invited her to take a drive with him. Clearly, after their first conversation, he had decided some sort of courtship was necessary to secure her fortune.

It was not, of course. She would obey her parents, as she always did, as she had always wanted to. Her current resentment had appeared from nowhere when her father had received a letter from Lord Maxwell, asking permission to pay Laura his addresses. And in the subsequent discussion on the subject between her parents and Oscar as though she were not even present. Only then did it strike her, how little choice she or any other girl of her class was given.

However she might rail against a fate in which she had no say, she had no intention of avoiding Lord Maxwell. She agreed with good grace to go with him in the gig and show him the countryside, providing the rain stayed off. Accordingly, wearing her new walking dress, she strolled out of the front door on his arm, while her mother smiled benignly and waved them off.

Laura prepared herself to comment on the weather, listen with fascination to monologues on whatever interested him, and laugh politely at his funny stories.

Instead, half-way down the driveway, he said, "Is Mrs. Lindon quite well?"

Laura turned toward him in surprise. "Of course. Or so I believe. What makes you ask?"

"Oh, I don't know. She does not seem quite as...effervescent as usual."

Laura smiled to hide her surge of anger. "I can only apologize if Mama has been backward in any attention. It is assuredly not her intention to make your lordship feel unwelcome. Quite the contrary."

Lord Maxwell turned the horses on to the road with easy skill. She was almost annoyed he didn't bump the gig against the gate.

"You really don't like me, do you, Miss Lindon?"

Her stomach jolted, and blood rushed up into her face. She had arrogantly assumed he would not understand she was insulting him. Hardly the behaviour of the obedient daughter or the perfect lady.

"I don't know you," she managed.

He glanced at her, a rueful smile in his eyes that was unexpectedly attractive. "But what you do know, you don't like. You may have heard something of my unsavoury reputation, which is mostly justified. I have sowed too many wild oats and must pay the price. There is no reason, however, why you should pay too."

She was so surprised she forgot to advise him to turn left at the crossroads and he drove straight on toward the main Trowbridge road.

"I am not sure I understand you, my lord," she said. Even more than when this marriage was first broached, she felt everything slipping from her control.

"I mean you are not bound to this marriage."

She stared at him. "You have agreed settlements with my father!"

"Which I will honour, should we choose to marry."

His eyes, the eyes of a rake and a drunkard, were surprisingly clear, and not stupid at all. She dropped her gaze hastily and found herself watching his hands instead, light and capable on the reins.

He said, "However, we don't *have* to marry. You will hate to be tied to a man you loathe and despise. And I will hate to have a wife who regards me so."

Emotion surged. Mostly it was confused shame. Some of it was definitely panic.

"You are jilting me?" she gasped.

His smile was twisted. "You really do have a low opinion of me. I would not do anything as ungentlemanly as jilting you. I merely point out that you have perfect grounds for jilting *me* if you so desire. Your family won't like it, of course, but I'll do my best to smooth things over before I go. No one will be terribly surprised, I assure you. I am a gazetted rake and fortune hunter."

Her jaw dropped in what must have been a most unbecoming manner. "You admit it?" she squeaked.

"Unworthy, Miss Lindon," he chided, his eyes mocking now, though whether her or himself was not clear. "We both know you are well aware of it. I had an expensive youth and seek to repair the damage. You are under no obligation to help me."

"I am," she whispered. Because it had all been arranged and she had agreed.

"I release you," he said, almost carelessly.

The world was crashing around her ears, and she had no idea what to do, what to say. What came out was unforgivably childish, and an echo of his own earlier observation. "You don't like me. I am not the lady you imagined."

He sighed. "Since we are, finally, being honest, I will admit that I barely thought of you at all. I admired you when we met last winter. I found you pretty, ladylike and with a charming hint of fun. And then I heard about the fortune you would inherit upon your marriage. It seemed perfect, so here I am. Only it's not so perfect, is it?"

She tried to laugh. "Because I am a shrew and do not pretend as well as I thought."

"Why should you? Mostly, you know, it is a matter of upbringing."

"It is?"

"Of course. You were brought up only to marry a suitable husband to oblige your family. I, like most men, was brought up to consider only myself. I do not even have the responsibilities of an eldest son, and I have been perfectly happy going to the devil."

His brows lifted in faint surprise. "Realization came to me only over the last couple of days—you don't have that choice, do you? You *can't* go the devil, or you are ostracized. You have no material means let alone society's permission to do other than obey your father and then your husband, however miserable you are."

He turned his gaze on her. "You don't have to say yes to me. Tell me to go and I will."

Relief should have flooded her. It was there, somewhere, but so was that inexplicable sense of panic. And then, out of nowhere, a horseman exploded into their path.

Their own horse reared, whinnying wildly while Laura clung to the side of the gig and Lord Maxwell tried to calm the startled horse. The other horseman caught it by the bridle in one hand. In the other, he held a pistol pointing very steadily at Lord Maxwell.

"Stand and deliver," the horseman said dangerously. He wore a baggy coat covered in stains that might have been blood, a floppy-brimmed hat pulled low over his forehead, and a large scarf pulled up to just beneath his eyes.

Laura's heart tried to jump into her mouth.

"Seriously?" Lord Maxwell said, apparently affronted. "On *this* little road?"

"Market day," the highwayman said. "People pass with money in their pockets."

"Do we look like people going to market?" Lord Maxwell demanded.

What was the matter with him? The highwayman had a pistol!

"None of your gab," the highwayman instructed with a ferocious frown. "Just hand over the money and the gew-gaws."

For a horrible moment, she thought Maxwell would argue the point. It crossed her mind that if she had not been present, he would have. Instead, he felt in his pockets and produced a coin purse.

The highwayman, urging his horse closer, snatched the purse. "Rolls of soft," he ordered.

"I don't bring such on a short drive with a lady."

Another scowl. "Ring, then. Watch," The pistol jerked toward Laura. "Lady's jewels."

"I don't wear them in the daytime," Laura said, glad to hear her voice remained steady.

The highwayman swore under his breath. "Bag," he growled.

Wordlessly, she passed her reticule to Lord Maxwell, who handed it to the highwayman. Did the pistol waver? Yes, it did and Lord Maxwell was watching... Oh God, he wasn't going to try and grab it, was he? One of them would be killed.

The highwayman stuffed his loot with apparent difficulty into his capacious pockets. "On your way," he snarled, then his eyes seemed to roll and he slumped suddenly over his horse's neck.

The pistol fell from his fingers and Lord Maxwell flung out his hand and caught it. Dropping it on the seat beside him, he leapt down from the gig, reached up and straightened the highwayman in the saddle before he fell off.

The highwayman's horse turned its head to look but didn't otherwise move. Lord Maxwell, reached with apparent distaste into the highwayman's pocket, and came out with Laura's crumpled reticule. He tossed it behind him into the gig, then returned to the highwayman's dubious coat for his signet ring and his purse, which he transferred to his own pocket before wiping his hands fastidiously on his handkerchief, unaccountably missed by the highwayman.

Then, to Laura's amazement, he reached up and shook the man. "Hello, Dick Turpin. Wake up."

The highwayman's eyes flickered and opened blearily.

"Go to a doctor, for God's sake," Lord Maxwell said in an annoyed voice. He shoved the reins into the highwayman's instinctively grasping fingers and hit the horse on the rump. "On your way," he said sternly.

Laura gasped as the highwayman's horse trotted away with him in the direction of Blanchester, and Lord Maxwell climbed calmly back into the gig. His gaze found hers. Unexpectedly, he reached for the hand in her lap and held it strongly. "There. We brushed through the adventure quite tolerably."

An involuntary frown of incomprehension began to tug at her brow. She didn't know if she was pleased or furious or frightened. Or all three. "You let him go."

"Felt sorry for him," Lord Maxwell admitted, slightly shame-faced. "Besides, we are on an expedition of pleasure, are we not?"

Speechless, she watched him as he urged the horse onward into a trot. She turned her head and saw the highwayman's horse galloping now, growing smaller and smaller into the distance.

"You felt sorry for him," she repeated, straightening to gaze once more at the elegant figure of Lord Maxwell. There was, it seemed rather more to this very odd man than she had guessed. "Is he ill?"

"Injured, I think. Possibly dying." His lips twisted into an apologetic smile. "He probably didn't start off a bad man, you know. Some injured sailors and soldiers invalided out can't find work and turn to crime to live. Some are too poor to have any choice if they want to survive."

"That isn't right," she said.

"No, it isn't."

"How do you know these things?"

He smiled. "I expect someone told me. Where is this lake of yours?"

"You missed the turning, but if you take the next track on the left we can get back there. The road is a bit rougher, but with pretty views."

"Excellent," Lord Maxwell said, and suddenly she wanted to laugh at his insouciance. Never once during the hold-up had he looked afraid or even troubled. For some reason, she found that uplifting.

A few minutes later, she remembered something else and turned to him. "That highwayman might have been the man who murdered your valet."

PIERS WAS SOMEWHAT disconcerted by the prospect of all the visitors Mrs. Lindon had invited to his home. For one thing, he had no idea who they were going to be and if he was supposed to recognize any of them. He understood they were mostly more distant neighbours invited for a few days stay, largely to entertain Lord Maxwell, and probably to help celebrate his betrothal to Laura. There was to be a ball at the end of their stay, to which Piers was invited, too.

I shall just have to be the haughty viscount, he thought sardonically, sitting back in his dining room chair when he had finished his soup. And surely his years of absence would be enough to account for his failure to recognize those he ought to. His immediate neighbours, he had found ways to remember, and in any case with increasing familiarity they had become easier to distinguish.

"Damn it," he said irritably, for he really wanted to spend tomorrow in the woods, looking again for clues as to who had been there with Nathaniel Orr. He might even find the missing bag.

"Damn what?" April said, taking his soup plate away.

Piers blinked in surprise, watching her remove the tureen from the table and then replace it with several covered dishes.

"It," he said unhelpfully. "Is this really one of your duties?"

"Oh, I'm just helping. Mavis scalded her hand and can't carry anything heavy."

"Mrs. Hicks told me we have footmen now."

"Two of 'em," April agreed. "But they're busy moving things around for tomorrow."

"What am I supposed to do with all these people tomorrow?"

"Feed them champagne and pretty bits of food. Cook has it in hand."

"Champagne?" he said, startled.

"Found several cases of it in the wine cellar. You should go down there some time. I read the label meself, even though it's got a *g* in there that didn't ought to be. Mrs. Hicks, and even Patrick the new first footman, reckon it will make you seem extravagantly hospitable and make you popular as—"

"Do they also reckon the champagne is drinkable?"

She grinned. "Want me to bring you some?"

"Better had." If his uncle hadn't drunk it, there had to be a reason.

In fact, it was the Patrick the footman who brought him the champagne, as well as the rest of his dinner, and it was indeed drinkable. Perhaps tomorrow wouldn't be so bad after all.

AS IT HAPPENED, THE sun shone for his impromptu garden party. After a morning with the estate books and Daniels, and a distracted luncheon spent mostly thinking about Orr, he found his overgrown garden transformed. The lawn was cut short and smooth, the borders of spring flowers had been weeded. A couple of tables set with white cloths and several chairs now stood in the shade of a willow tree. More had been placed on the terrace. And beneath an awning, were set out the champagne bottles and glasses, alongside other drinks.

A Spanish guitar stood casually propped up against the wall, presumably for whoever wished to entertain the company. Distractedly Piers picked it up and wandered onto the lawn, where an old pall mall set was laid out. Sitting down by the willow, he gazed around him.

One strum of the guitar was enough to make him wince. He set about tuning it.

Mrs. Hicks bustled over to him. "What do you think?" she asked anxiously.

"I think you've worked a miracle," he said warmly. "I'd never have thought of using the garden. Excellent idea."

He spared her a glance from the guitar and saw a brief struggle wage across her face.

"It was April's idea," she said at last. "And to be fair, she did most of the organizing and the work out here."

Surprised, he let his gaze drop to the guitar once more. "A fine decision," he said vaguely. "Where did the guitar come from?"

"Miss Maria used to play it occasionally. She has a better one now, she tells me. A wedding gift from Mr. Gadsby."

"I'm glad he is so thoughtful." He thought he heard the sounds of carriage wheels across gravel and strummed again to keep out the noise.

"That must be your guests arriving," Mrs. Hicks said, wiping her hands on her dress.

She was nervous, too. It must have been years since she had catered for any entertaining here.

He put the guitar down, now that it no longer hurt his ears. "You run a tight household, Mrs. Hicks. We shall do well."

He stood, drawing the invisible mantle of the viscount around him, and strolled around the side of the house to greet his guests.

There were several carriages full of them, led by Mrs. Lindon, Laura and Lord Maxwell.

"Lord Petteril!" Mrs. Lindon exclaimed, advancing upon him as soon as she was handed down from the carriage. She extended her hand gracefully.

It was odd, but she no longer looked so ridiculously young for her years. The fine lines at her eyes and mouth seemed more deeply etched, her face curiously less defined, as though the anxiety of her daughter's approaching nuptials had finally touched her.

"How kind of you to invite us at such short notice." She seemed to have forgotten she had done all the inviting. "I've been telling our guests all about your beautiful house. Don't you find its proportions unusually pleasing, Lord Maxwell?"

She still held on to Petteril's hand while Maxwell answered, "Very fine architecture, Petteril."

"Thank you, but I can take no credit."

Mrs. Lindon cast him a quick, laughing glance which almost banished the impression of ageing, and let his hand slip away. She turned to introduce him to a blur of people, some of whom had names he recalled very vaguely but most of whom were complete strangers.

Patrick the first footman was waiting to conduct them around to the garden rather than through the front door, which caused a fresh burst of excitement from the younger ladies, all chattering at once.

Lindon laid his hand on Piers's arm. "Got something to show you," he said. "It will only take a moment."

Since Mrs. Lindon had invited everyone, Piers felt no guilt in abandoning her to entertain them, while he led Lindon inside. Lord Maxwell came, too. Piers took them into the estate office, since it was the nearest place with privacy, and shut the door.

From the pocket of his loose-fitting country coat, Lindon removed something wrapped in cloth and laid it on the desk. Like a conjurer, he unwrapped the cloth and revealed an old, scratched pistol.

"Belongs to the highwayman," Lindon said dramatically. "My daughter and Hunter here were held up by him yesterday."

Piers's eyes widened, flying immediately to Hunter. "I'm grateful to see you both unhurt! What happened?"

"He was waiting behind a hedge, I think, just this side of the main road to Trowbridge. At any rate, he and his horse suddenly appeared in front of us, and he forced our horse to halt." He nodded at the pistol.

"He pointed *that* at us and demanded our valuables – of which there were few enough, considering. He was hoping for someone with pockets full of coin for the market. At any rate, we gave him what we had, and then he sort of collapsed over his horse's neck and dropped the pistol. I got out and picked it up, then took back our things and we drove off."

"Had a pic-nick," Lindon said with a hint of admiration for such savoir faire.

"I admire Miss Lindon's courage," Piers murmured.

"So do I," Maxwell said. "No sign of the vapours whatsoever."

"Thing is," Lindon said, "the pistol wasn't loaded."

"I suppose he finds the threat of it is enough for his purpose."

"Certainly, but suppose he found on one occasion that it wasn't?" Lindon said with impatient excitement.

Piers turned to him. "Such as against Orr?" he said slowly. "Hence he had to use the hunting knife." He frowned, swinging back to Hunter. "I don't suppose the knife was Orr's?"

"I've never seen it before," Hunter said. "But it could have been his. I suppose he could have carried it with him for defence since he was traveling at night."

"I wish we knew *why* he was traveling at night," Piers said. "I feel it would solve the whole mystery. Shall I lock this up here to save your carrying it around all afternoon?" With Lindon's nod of agreement, he swept the pistol into the desk drawer, turned the key and pocketed it. "What was he like, this highwayman?" he asked Hunter.

Lord Maxwell did not quite tug at his cravat, but he did look vaguely uncomfortable. "Desperate. Sick."

"Was he young or old? Fat or thin?"

"Hard to tell his age, never saw much except his eyes. He was thin and grubby."

"Doesn't sound much like Brandy Bill, does it?" Lindon sad ruefully.

"Could be Brandy Bill with Alleyn's pistol ball still lodged in his body." Piers met Hunter's gaze. "Is he dying?"

"I suspect so."

Which meant they may not have long to find him and discover what, if anything, he had to do with Orr's death. But Hunter's discomfort intrigued Piers. It was almost as if he felt sorry for the highwayman, and yet was half-ashamed of letting him go when he had had the man at his mercy. On the other hand, he had also been in company with a young lady whom he certainly would not have wanted to risk in any fight with a desperate criminal.

"Best join our guests," Piers said, "or they'll think I'm even more eccentric."

"Even more eccentric than what?" Hunter asked, amused.

"Afraid it's us being eccentric," Lindon said, colouring as he made for the door. "Sorry about this, Petteril. Afraid Evangela got rather carried away and inflicted us all on you without invitation. I told her it was not the thing—in fact, downright rude—especially when you don't have a hostess."

"Not at all," Pies said politely. "Very happy to meet all the neighbours. And Mrs. Lindon assured me she would act as hostess." Though she hadn't offered to pay for the food now being carried up from the kitchen, or for the cases of champagne being glugged in the garden.

Chapter Nine

I n fact, Piers was amused now, rather than annoyed, and even pleased to have the opportunity of observing his neighbours, in particular those who might know something about Orr's death. While Mrs. Lindon was so delighted by the charming little garden party that she rushed up immediately to tell him so.

Surprise lurked amidst the admiration in her eyes, forcing him to confess, "Actually, it was my housekeeper and my assistant who arranged it all. But I'm glad it meets with your approval. You have a larger task, entertaining so many for so long."

She laughed, a rather pleasant, throaty sound, which lent her a vitality and a friendliness he had not detected before. She really must have been pleased with his party, for she took his arm. "Come, let me introduce you to some of your more distant neighbours."

Of course, he had no hope of ever distinguishing between so many faces, so the viscount he had learned to play developed a new facet of benign hospitality. He strolled among his guests with hand shakes and bows and a smile so fixed to his lips that his jaw began to ache. After a while, he stopped shaking hands and merely smiled and nodded.

His new footmen circulated among the guests with plates of small pastries, tiny sandwiches, and other treats that could be consumed in a bite or two. The maids—among them the unmistakable, slight figure of April in her old-fashioned blue dress and white cap over glimmering of bright, golden hair—refilled glasses, swept up abandoned crockery and bits of food, and fetched and carried whatever was required. Piers was proud of them and made a mental note to send them his praise and thanks.

Finding himself momentarily alone, he propped his shoulder against the trunk of a shady tree and watched the young people playing pall mall. Among them were Laura Lindon and Lord Maxwell, bickering more like brother-and-sister than a betrothed couple. At least the terrible tension between them seemed to have vanished.

Piers became aware of someone standing next to him, gazing in the same direction though with considerably less pleasure. Samuel Alleyn, who didn't even seem to be aware of Piers's presence.

"Mr. Alleyn," he said politely. "Pall mall not to your liking? Or are you waiting for the next game?"

Samuel looked startled. "I'm afraid I am not very good at leisure. My cast of mind is too serious, or so I am told."

"Perhaps your idea of leisure is merely somewhat quieter," Piers suggested, provoking something almost like a smile from Samuel, whose gaze turned curious,

"Yours also, I imagine," he said. "Is it true that you were an Oxford don before you inherited the title?"

"I was. Still would be, from choice. It is not a course *you* chose to follow?"

Samuel's lips twisted very slightly. "It was not the choice I was given. My father admires education, but only as a hobby. It does not make money." He must have realized that he had betrayed disrespect for his parent, for he flushed, and rushed on. "My choice was between going into our business in the north or becoming a gentleman farmer here. So I chose the latter."

"From our conversation at Barnwood, it is a very successful choice. Your land thrives as I am hoping mine will in time."

Samuel looked gratified, although his gaze quickly strayed back to Laura who was squabbling with Lord Maxwell over a mallet. Hunter laughed and gave it up with a mocking bow, to which she replied with a triumphant and not entirely serious toss of her lovely head.

Samuel winced. There was nothing Piers could say that would help. He remembered the unbearable pangs of first love and jealousy only too well. But there was no denying Samuel's feeling for Laura was strong. Strong enough to kill Hunter to have a chance with her? And then, appalled that he had killed the wrong man, to try and cover his deed?

It was possible. Emotion ran high in him. He had the passion. But to Piers, he did not appear the kind to stab a man in the dark. Years of withstanding the condescension of his supposed friends seemed to have lent him a hard edge, a courage that would lead him to direct confrontation, whatever the cost to his dignity.

His father, on the other hand, was outwardly amiable, inwardly steely. A man who must have been prepared to do anything to make his business thrive and prosper, earning him enough to buy a country estate, and an expensive education for his son. One didn't earn such money without ruthlessness and risk.

Samuel moved away, as though the sight of Laura was unbearable. Piers watched him go, and beyond him observed Mrs. Lindon, deigning to smile upon one of the footmen who had offered her a glass. Piers was glad for his sake of her appreciation.

"Champagne, my lord?" April's voice said at his side, causing him to blink at her in surprise.

"I seem to have lost my glass. Mrs. Hicks tell me much of this is your doing."

"Do you mind?" she asked, her eyes wary.

He smiled. "Of course not. It is an excellent idea and appears to be highly popular. Easier to observe people also."

"That's what I thought. Interesting, isn't it?" She darted away and came back with a filled glass for him.

"Thank you."

"So what have you observed?"

"Nothing immediately helpful," he admitted. "Beyond the un-loaded pistol of our local highwayman. He held up Hunter and Laura yesterday."

"So I heard."

"You can tell me your observations later," he murmured, moving away toward a group of guests he had no names for.

A little after that, as the tables were set with tea and scones and cakes, he came upon Laura, seated alone with the guitar on her knee.

"Do you play?" he asked.

She threw him a quick smile. "I was just trying to remember if I could. Miss Withan tried to teach me when I was an admiring, wide-eyed child. She played beautifully."

"Maria?" He dredged his mind for musical memories of his cousin, the late viscount's elder daughter. "I never heard her play."

She strummed gently and smiled at the pleasing sound. "It gets lost, I think, in the determination to shine at the pianoforte. But this has a more...wild, exotic sound, don't you find?"

He considered. "I expect it depends who is playing."

Her lips quirked. "A metaphor for life," she murmured, then laughed and set down the guitar. "No, it seems I cannot remember where to put my silly fingers." Her gaze went beyond him. "Sam, you've brought me tea, which is exactly what I want."

Tactfully, Piers moved away, but Samuel was granted only a moment alone with Laura before her mother appeared, closely followed by several other young people and he moved quietly away.

A few minutes later, he found Oscar pouring the last remains of a champagne bottle into his glass, while gazing across the lawn at his sister's lively table.

"Tell me, Piers," Oscar said, "what do you honestly think of Hunter?"

Piers. So they were back to boyhood equality. "I honestly think it's a little late to chase character references."

"They wouldn't be great, would they?" Oscar said ruefully.

"Your parents must have known what he was before he offered for Laura."

"The reality is a little more daunting. Before he came, it was as if he was merely a wooden figure attached to all these other important figures. I want to go into politics, you know, win a seat in parliament."

"Then the Hunter influence will be useful."

"Are you interested in politics, Petteril?"

"I wasn't. I probably am now." Then, since Oscar appeared to expect more, he added, "There is much that needs to change."

Oscar nodded, apparently pleased, but reverted suddenly to Hunter. "Do you believe he would look after Laura? Make her a good husband?"

"He seems to have looked after her when they met Brandy Bill," Piers said mildly. "Beyond that, you are asking the wrong man." He turned away just in time to be besieged by three young ladies he could not tell apart from each other or from anyone else.

"My lord, we are playing one more game of pall mall before we have to go. Do say you will be on our side!"

"Only if Mr. Lindon captains the other team," Piers said, submitting to being led off with a girl on either arm, while the third all but hauled Oscar along beside them.

An hour later, they were all gone and Piers, for the sake of sanity, shut himself up in the library with his books to revel in peace and solitude and soothe his jangling nerves.

Throwing his coat over the back of an upright chair, he grabbed a book at random off the nearest shelf, tugged off his cravat and threw himself into the comfortable chair by the unlit fire. For a while he just sat there, with the book unopened on his knee, breathing in and out and letting the waves of foolish tension trickle off him.

At last, he put on his reading glasses and opened the book. At almost the same time, the library door opened, and he knew a powerful urge to hurl the book at whoever had come in. Restraining the impulse, he sat still, hoping whoever it was would go away.

April materialized in front of him bearing a glass of brandy, which she set down wordlessly on the small table beside him. As though she had taken in his mood at a glance—how did she even know a brandy was just what he wanted when he hadn't even known it himself?—she turned immediately to go. And suddenly, he couldn't bear the loneliness.

"Stay," he said aloud, before he could control it. At once, she turned back, surprise in her face, and curiosity not unmixed with apprehension. "If you have time," he added, almost painfully, aware that the servants would now be clearing up in the garden.

Her brow twitched, but she dragged the footstool over and sat on it, not quite at his feet but close enough. It was odd, even incomprehensible how the presence of this little creature, this scrap of frequently criminal humanity from the gutter who caused him so many problems, soothed his spirit when even solitude could not.

Something else to think about when she was not here, for it connected in his mind with that devastating glimpse of her in the attic of the London house. She had danced in a beam of sunlight that pierced the tiny, grubby window, laughing at herself with all the enjoyment of a child dressing up and all the grace of a unique and lovely woman.

He had never met anyone so adaptable. He waited until the attic memory faded into the time spent here at Haybury before he lifted his gaze to her face, wondering what to say to explain his inexplicable need of her presence. But it seemed he didn't need to say anything. She was gazing beyond him to the window and the formal garden. Her posture was relaxed, her expression contented, almost as though she shared the peculiar peace of the moment.

So, he took a sip of his brandy, letting his mind dwell where it would.

He said, "How have you been getting on with your inspection of the public rooms?"

She delved into the pouch at her waist and produced her notebook. She opened it and passed it over to him. "Can you read it?"

Touched by her self-consciousness, he nodded. Her writing looked like that of a child and veered up and down like a caterpillar, but the letters were recognizable and clear. He was proud of her. "I'll keep it with me, if you won't miss it tonight?"

She nodded and straightened slightly, as though pleased he found her work of value. "Did you learn anything from watching the nobs this afternoon?" she asked.

"Not much that is new," he replied ruefully, "though I suppose it clarified and emphasized some things in my mind. Samuel and Oscar are both ambitious in their own ways: Samuel for the acceptance of the gentry, and the hope of Laura Lindon; Oscar for a higher status than a mere country squire. I wouldn't be surprised if it wasn't he rather than his father who most sought the marriage alliance between Laura and Hunter." He frowned. "He seems to be cooling on the match, now, though. I wonder why? Do you suppose he suspects Hunter of killing the valet?"

She cast him an odd look. "More likely, he's noticed you would be just as good."

Startled, he sat up and the book slid off his knee. April caught it. "Me?" he said, appalled.

"You're the viscount, remember? And Hunter's a rake and a younger son. He prob'ly saw the other girls flirting with you and realized the prize."

Piers stared at her. "Flirting?" he said cautiously and now her eyes laughed at him.

"Didn't you notice?"

"No," he said, though recalling the smiles and the pall mall abduction, he should have.

"Even Mrs. Lindon. Though I wouldn't take that too seriously. She flirts with everyone."

"*Mrs. Lindon?*"

She ignored that. "Trouble is, no one has any motive to kill Orr. Unless he was blackmailing someone, and they all seem too dull and respectable for that."

"Yes... But then, I don't really know them. I was only a boy the last time I saw these people and anything could have happened since. I wrote to Peter Haggard and Gussie to see what they know of anyone concerned. And to Pepper to see if he can find anything to Orr's discredit. But if Hunter was the intended victim..."

"Then we got too many suspects. Samuel to get rid of his rival, Laura to get rid of a husband she doesn't want, Oscar to help her since he may already have decided he'd prefer you. Mr. Lindon for the same reason?"

"Or do we acquit him since he's the magistrate? I'd swear he is far too appalled by having to deal with it all for him to have caused the whole upset."

"Mrs. Lindon, then."

An ugly idea entered his head. "She *is* a flirt," he said slowly. "What if she was having an affair with Hunter and couldn't bear that he was marrying her daughter?"

"She makes the assignation in the wood, but Hunter sends his man to tell her it's over. She kills him before she realizes he's not Hunter." She scowled. "Only why burn his clothes?"

Piers nodded. "And Hunter, in honour, could not tell anyone what really happened... It's possible... There's a determination, a strength in her that could make her capable of murder. And yet I cannot imagine..."

"What?"

"Hunter. He's a privileged ne'er-do-well, but I can't imagine him agreeing to marry the daughter if he had ever had an affair with the mother. He would consider it...uncivil."

"Would killing Orr be uncivil too?" April asked with an edge of sarcasm.

"Yes, I think so ," he replied seriously. "For the same reason he doesn't seduce maids. He's in a position of power and it wouldn't be right."

"Don't stop most of 'em," she said, curling her lip.

"No, probably not." He spread his fingers and counted them off. "So we think Mrs. Lindon is capable of murder. For my money, so is Oscar. And both male Alleyns."

"And Brandy Bill," April reminded him.

"Is he?" Piers wondered. "He didn't even load his pistol when he took to the high toby."

"Perhaps he just ran out of ammunition and couldn't afford more. Or was too afraid to buy it in Blanchester in case he was recognized."

"True." Piers sighed, and let his hand drop to his lap. He reached for the brandy again, then lowered the glass before it touched his lips. "On the other hand, Hunter let him go. If he runs to form, then that's because he recognized the highwayman was weaker than him."

"He was. He was unconscious and about to fall off his horse." Her breath caught. "What if there was some kind of alliance between Hunter and Brandy Bill? Orr found out, so Hunter set him up for Bill to do him in. And now Hunter's helping Bill, if only to keep him away from the authorities and any discovery of their connection."

Piers scratched the back of his head. "Seems a bit fanciful. I can't see Hunter in the role. The truth is, we need to speak to Brandy Bill."

April nodded agreement. "You got time tomorrow?"

He wrinkled his nose. "It's Sunday. No reading lessons... But I'd better go to church in the morning to please the locals. I'd rather have the whole day to track down Bill, or someone might warn him we're looking and scare him off somewhere else entirely. Besides, I can't help feeling there's more to learn from the woods."

"Maybe," she said non-commitally. "We haven't even considered servants or other ordinary folk. Any of them could have known Orr and had some reason to hate him."

"True. But they would surely be more inclined to sell his clothes and his boots rather than burn them. Burning them speaks of hatred to me."

"Hatred ain't limited to the nobs."

He focused his gaze on her. "Do you have someone particular in mind? You know the servants better than I do."

She shook her head, jumping to her feet as though ashamed to have brought the subject of the servants up. "Nah. Just thinking aloud. I'd better go and help clear up."

He nodded, watching her go. Only at the last minute did he say, "April? You did well setting up this party. Another unexpected talent."

She blushed, but he thought beneath the embarrassment she was pleased. And that made him smile.

Chapter Ten

April's plan worked perfectly the following morning. Benson harnessed the pony to the kitchen gig for her. Since this was Sunday, Cook would not need the vehicle today. The servants all walked to church in the village.

"Thanks, Mr. Benson," April said, climbing up with her carpet bag. "You won't say a word to himself, will you?"

"Not unless he asks me," he said warningly. "But then I will. *You* should tell him."

"I will after. It's just he won't let me go alone."

"And you don't think there's a good reason for that?"

"I'm safer without him," she said stubbornly. "You know I always looked after myself."

"And I know you were pleased enough to sleep somewhere decent of a night," he retorted.

"I'll be back well before I need to think of sleep," she said, deliberately misunderstanding him. "Thanks, Mr. B!"

Handling the pony was both easier and more boring than the exhilaration of driving the greys in the curricle, but at least it trotted along at a fair clip. Lord Petteril would go in the other direction to church, so she didn't fear running into him. The worst part of the journey, in fact, was when she left the pony and gig and walked alone into the wood.

There, with the hair standing up on the back of her neck, and glancing constantly all around her, she whipped off her petticoats and linen cap, and climbed into Ape's breeches and loose old jacket, and crammed her hair beneath the familiar cap. Then she stuffed April's clothes into the bag. She took a handful of dirt, rubbed her hands together then wiped them over her clothes and her face while creeping back through the trees toward the gig.

Breathing a sigh of relief to be out of the trees, she finally remembered she should not be creeping like a nervous girl but swaggering like a fearless boy. She had almost forgotten how. In fact, the boy's clothes felt surprisingly unfamiliar, even strange. And yet it had been less than a week since she'd last worn them, It seemed she had become a girl again much more easily than she had expected. She still wasn't sure she liked it, and she definitely rejoiced in her freedom of movement now she no longer had the weight of skirts around her legs.

She strode up to the pony, gave him a piece of carrot for his patience, and leapt back up into the gig, where she sat with her knees apart and grinned as she urged the pony into a trot and set off again for Blanchester.

She made good time to the inn in Blanchester where Orr's inquest had been held, and left the pony and gig there before following her nose to the less salubrious parts of town. A weird sense of familiarity twisted at her stomach as she moved deeper into the narrower streets. The alleys of damp, crumbling buildings, the hopeless faces, the smells of human waste and rotting food, were just the same. So were the threats, brazen or hidden, and she did not know these streets the way she knew St. Giles, or the patch of the riverside she had survived on before that.

Because everything was on a smaller scale, she stood out all the more easily as a stranger. So, fighting a novel sense of guilt and pity that threatened to distract her, she set about establishing her reasons for being there. She pestered people, asking for work, dipping in and out of alehouses, asking the few street sellers when she bought a wrinkled apple and a stale pie for very little money.

"Got any doctors round here then?" she asked the pie seller after he had refused her offer to work for him for the day. He wasn't exactly run off his feet with custom. "I worked for a doctor once."

"Don't be daft," the pie seller scoffed.

"Or I could look after sick people myself," April said, straightening as though the thought had just struck her. "Know any sick people, mister?"

"'Course I do. But none as could pay you to mop their fevered brow."

"Not even for the price of a meal a day?" she asked, disappointed. "Someone who ain't got no family. I could get their food in and such, too..."

"You're daft," the seller said frankly. "You're not from round here, nether."

"Nah. Come from London." She grinned cheekily. "Had a spot of bother there and fancied a change of scene."

"Well, you're not welcome here, so shab off."

She shabbed off and repeated her story a couple more times, to a washer woman coming out of her doorway, and then to an idle man propping up a filthy street corner, and got much the same response. Though the idle man who was young and bored added, "There's no work round here. None that won't get you lifted by the law, anyway."

"I ain't thieving," April said self-righteously. "Not for anything. Had enough of that. Ain't worth it."

"It ain't," the lounging man agreed morosely. He looked at April. "What's it like in London, then? There work there?"

"More chance than here," April said, tearing off a chunk of the unappetising pie and offering it to him in a companionable sort of way. "But it's hard to get respectable-like, if you don't know someone as can give you a character." She looked him up and down. "You could get work at the docks, I expect. I'm too small, but you look strong enough."

"Yes?" The man took her scrap of pie with a nod of acknowledgement. "Might just do that." He chewed the pie and swallowed without grimacing, which was more than April felt capable of, and eyed her. "If you're desperate, speak to the man with the red hat band down the next street."

"Why, what's he do?"

"Ask him," the idle man replied dryly, aiming a friendly slap at her head. April ducked, grinned at him and dashed off in the direction he indicated.

The man in the red hat band was not immediately apparent, mainly due to the fact that the band was so grubby it wasn't very obviously red. But eventually, when the street emptied of everyone except her and one portly man sitting on a doorstep with an old leather flask, she swaggered over to ask him. And finally saw that his hat band was still red in places.

"Someone said you might have a job for me," she said hopefully.

"And who are you?" the man said with contempt.

"Who are *you*?" she countered. "And what's the job?"

Half-heartedly, he aimed a kick at her. "Do I look like a man with staff?"

"Well, you ain't doing anything yourself."

"You're a cheeky little bugger."

"Yes, but I work hard, And I'll do anything. Anything honest," she added. "What you got?"

"What do you think?"

"I think you're bored," April said frankly. "And I think you want to go the alehouse 'cause your flask's empty. Ain't you got no money?"

"'Course I got money, you little—"

She let her eyes widen. "You working now, mister? *Right* now?"

He pushed his hat to the back of his head. "Might be... Tell you what, bright little fellow, I'll give you a penny to sit here until I get back. All you got to do is look out for the law."

"What do I do if I sees 'em?"

"Tell 'em the bloke upstairs is your da who got bit by a dog and can't get out of bed."

April's heart lurched with hope. "Is he *your* da?"

The red hat band stood up, wheezing out a laugh. "Yes, he's my da and you're standing in as his boy. If you gets warning as the constables are coming this way, you could warn him, but he ain't moving so fast, so might be best to brazen it out." He took a penny from his pocket and held it up. "Want it?"

April considered. "I'll take two,"

He tossed her the penny. "You'll get the second when I come back. If he's still here and still alive."

It would never have been that easy in St, Giles, April reflected, not if she didn't know anyone. Then it struck her that it was so easy because he of the red hat band didn't believe his job would last long anyway. His employer was dying.

April forced herself to lounge on the step for several minutes after the man vanished from view. Then she turned and went in.

The smell was choking. How quickly she'd got used to comfort and freshness and the ways of the rich... There was nowhere to go but up the stairs, two flights. The door at the top wasn't even properly closed, never mind locked. If Brandy Bill the highwayman really was on the other side of it, was he too ill to care? Or was it Red Hatband who didn't care, considered his employer a lost cause and only hung around to claim his possessions when he finally croaked?

For a moment, she hesitated. She didn't want to be shot just because she took someone by surprise.

"Hello?" she called, knocking softly on the door before she pushed it further open. The smell of unwashed body was powerful, but she forced herself to go in.

The room was small and gloomy, partly because the window was so dirty, but she saw at once why someone like the highwayman might have picked it. A narrow iron stair ran from the roof across the window, no doubt leading to the ground or at least to a lower floor. The rest of the building was probably used for sweat shops and store rooms. But from here, there was definitely another way out.

The room itself contained only a table—on which resided a jug, half a stale loaf and a sad hunk of cheese—a hard chair, a small chest of drawers, an ancient stove, and a bed.

April stopped dead. In the bed, wearing an incongruously frilly nightcap, a very ugly and outraged old woman lay glaring at her.

AFTER CHURCH, PIERS managed to avoid most of the chatter in the yard and all of the invitations being flung his way and drove home to swap the greys for the Professor, duly saddled. At last, he was able to follow the nagging of his mind to Petteril Wood.

This time, instead of exploring the area closest to the Dog and Duck and Blanchester, he walked around the wood nearest to the house.

Memory drew him to what he and his brother and cousins had called "the cave". It had been a great place to play at being Robin Hood or more evil bandits. Of course, it was less a cave than a hollow formed in a slope, half-covered by tree roots. Even as boys, only a couple of them could fit in to shelter from the rain, and their feet had always stuck out.

But someone had done better. They had rigged an extension from the top of the hollow, made of branches and leaves. And near that were the remains of a campfire. With a growing sense of excitement, he lay under the shelter and crawled into the hollow.

Annoyingly, it was empty.

He wriggled half out again and paused, eyeing a dark spot on one of the roots. Piers shifted to let more light in, even eased out his quizzing glass to inspect the stain more closely. It still looked like blood. As though someone had brushed a wound against it. Piers pushed the rest of the way out and sat up, considering.

Someone had camped out here. He could still see the blackened remains of a fire. It could have been poachers, village children, anyone, really. But his money was on Brandy Bill, already injured, no doubt from Mr. Alleyn's reaction to being held up. Something had then driven the highwayman from his shelter. Petteril's own return? Or the arrival of Nathaniel Orr?

Could it really be as simple as that? The highwayman shot the perceived threat to his presence here?

Only, why burn Orr's clothes?

He stood, remounted, and rode back toward the house.

"Send April to me in the library," he instructed the footman who let him in. He hadn't yet learned to distinguish between them.

"As soon as she returns, my lord."

"Returns?" He paused, frowning at the footman. "From where?"

"I don't know, my lord, but she's not in the house. Shall I run and ask Mrs. Hicks? She will know."

Piers doubted it. "No, don't worry. I'll find her when I need to." He walked straight on and out again by the side door that was nearest to the stables.

There, he ascertained that the kitchen pony had gone. And no doubt the little gig that it pulled. A shadow fell over him.

"Want the Professor again?" Benson asked in surprise.

"Where is April?"

Benson sighed. "She don't want me to tell you."

"If I say she's gone to Blanchester in search of a highwayman whom I'm very afraid she will find?"

Benson paled. "Oh, Gawd, she didn't say anything about a highwayman. But she did go off to Blanchester."

Piers held his gaze. "In her blue dress?"

"Yes, my lord," Benson mumbled. "Shall I fetch her back?"

Piers turned on his heels. "I doubt you could find her. Harness the greys again, will you?"

Back in the house, he took the stairs three at a time, more to be rid of the build up of fearful energy inside him than because saving a few seconds would make any difference to finding her.

Stewart was in the dressing room, putting away Piers's freshly laundered shirts.

"Bring me that bag up there, would you?" Piers pointed to the top of the wardrobe, then strode back to the bedroom, throwing off his coat and cravat as he went. He sat on the bed to haul off his boots, and a second later found the bag beside him and Stewart kneeling to pull off the boots for him.

"Thanks," Piers muttered. "That will be all for now."

Stewart bowed silently and departed, leaving Piers to open the bag and take out the old coat, shirt, boots, and pantaloons that he had stuffed in there on impulse before leaving London. Just in case he might need them.

The hat looked even more battered after the journey, but no doubt this was all to the good. He swung the traveling cloak around his shoulders and, carrying the hat, ran back downstairs to the front door, where Benson waited with the greys.

"Want me with you, sir?" the groom asked, passing the reins.

Piers flashed him a quick smile of gratitude. "No, you're too respectable."

APRIL, CONFRONTED BY the unexpected sight of the frilly old woman, thought fast. "You'll be the sick lady. I'm here to help."

A look of sardonic amusement pierced the fevered eyes. April risked a smile and a few steps nearer, where she made another discovery. The old woman didn't just have an incipient moustache, her whole jaw and chin were covered in stubble.

She laughed. "Gawd, I should have spotted that one. Afternoon, Mr. Bill."

Brandy Bill snatched off the nightcap and shoved it under his grimy pillow. His hand shook. "Where's Alf?" he croaked.

"Red Hatband? He had to go to the alehouse, paid me to watch instead."

"Then what you doing up here?"

For a moment there was a threat, a frightening violence in his eyes that stung April's stomach with healthy fear. But apparently, the expression was too much effort to maintain because it faded very fast.

April swallowed. "I don't want you to die."

"What's it to you?"

"I need to know something, But I can clean your wound first and get you some decent food."

"What wound? I'm sick."

"Then I'll clean that. Mr. Alleyn shot you on the Trowbridge road when you held him up, and everyone knows it's not getting any better."

Bill tried to sneer, but it was clear he was in considerable pain, and she had the impression the world seemed very far away for him. Still, he tried. "That right? And how does *everyone* know that?"

"'Cause you held up Lord Maxwell and the magistrate's daughter and fainted."

"Magistrate's daughter?" he repeated in appalled tones. His eyes closed. "Nothing to do with me. Gentlemen of the high toby don't faint."

"Not unless they're hurt, I expect," April said with as much understanding as she could muster.

The highwayman forced his eyes open again. "Who in hell's fires are you and what do you want?"

"Ape. I want to know if you stabbed Nathaniel Orr."

She had hoped to take him by surprise and learn something, but he was really too befuddled to take anything in very quickly. There was a definite pause before he said virtuously, "Never stabbed anyone since I come home."

"Home? Blanchester is your home?"

"Christ, no. Miserable, mean little dump. I mean home in England."

Her eyes widened. "You a sailor? Soldier?"

"I was. Got shot through the leg and couldn't run. So they sent me home. I can ride pretty good."

"I suppose you need to in your profession."

He glowered at her. "You trying to trick me?"

"No." April scowled back, then scolded. "Tell you something else for free. You shouldn't trust that red hatband cove. He didn't even shut your door, never mind lock it, and I reckon he'd run at the first whisper of trouble and never mind warning you neither."

A hint of a weary smile passed over Bill's face. "Can't get the staff, don't you know," he said a very poor imitation of a nob's accent. "I should take my chances alone. Old habits die hard, I suppose...got to post your pickets."

April sat down on his bed. She couldn't smell the corruption she'd come across in other injured people who had lost limbs or just died of it. But this man undeniably needed a wash. "Let's see, then. I'll swap you my help for information. Where is it?"

He moved the grimy blanket and revealed the bandage around his chest. He touched his side, just under his arm. Blood had seeped through the bandage. "The ball ain't in there. Come out the other side. And I knows enough to keep it clean."

She doubted he could reach both sides of the wound. Still, he let her unwind the bandage and look, and sure enough, the smaller wound at the back was surrounded by an angry red, puffy area.

"Got any brandy?" she asked.

He grimaced and produced a bottle from the other side of the bed. "Can't afford brandy in rough times. Gin Bill doesn't have the same ring, though, does it?"

"Expect it does the same job," she said. "Hold on to the bed clothes."

Pouring gin over both wounds turned his grey skin white and she thought he might even have fainted again. Which at least gave her the opportunity to creep out onto the landing, remove her jacket and tear her shirt into strips for clean bandages. Then she fastened her loose jacket very carefully to the top button, and went back into the room.

She managed to rebind the wound and help prop him more comfortably against the pillows. She was just giving him a cup of ale from the jug on the table when she became aware of movement on the stairs.

The hairs prickled on the back of her neck, but she forced herself to stay where she was, watching Bill sip the ale. His colour was no longer quite so frightening, so she glanced up with studied casualness as the door burst open.

Red Hatband, known to the highwayman as Alf, stood there, staring. His threatening presence seemed to fill the room, and his angry gaze was on April.

"What are you doing in here?" he demanded.

"Looking after him," she said.

"Looks to me like you're trying to muscle in on my job. After I did you a favour, too. Scarper."

April was furious. She hadn't even had the chance to ask Bill what she had come for, and this oaf was dismissing her. Biting her tongue, she managed to say, "I'd rather earn my other penny. Going to get him something to eat now."

"There's only the bread and cheese," Alf sneered. "Just put it where he can reach it."

"No wonder he ain't better," April said darkly. "You should have brought him some soup or stew from the tavern."

Alf sneered. "Why don't you get it with the penny I gave you?"

April rose to her feet, her heart thudding as he advanced on her. "'Cause that's my penny and I don't trust you to give me another," she said, trying desperately to keep in character.

Alf raised his hand, the back of it toward her face. "Scarper," he said again. "Hop it. Shab off."

"Let him be," Bill growled. "Go get me some decent food. There's a purse still in the drawer."

Alf grinned. "No, there ain't, matey. And Brandy Bill, ain't so scary as a corpse neither."

"I ain't dead yet," Bill said, rearing up on his pillows.

Alf laughed and took a vicious swipe at April with the back of his hand. April, who had been dodging blows all her life, ducked easily. Her survival instinct told her to bolt immediately to the door, but she didn't trust Alf not to kill Bill now that the highwayman was so weak, and she remained standing defiantly between Alf and the bed.

Bill raised the gin bottle in his good hand, ready to smash it on Alf's head, but Alf jerked around and snatched it, spinning right around to strike April with it instead. Desperately, she flung up her arm to protect her face, and tensed for the inevitable blow.

"Stop," commanded a voice from the doorway.

Chapter Eleven

*H*ow the devil...?

The voice and the command were those of the imperious viscount, but when April peered over her sleeve and the others froze, all eyes on the man striding into the room, the speaker was a much seedier character.

He wore a battered hat, spectacles, and a once good but in-need-of-mending coat. His shirt cuffs were badly ink stained, and his boots were polished but down-at-heel. He carried a cane which had slid apart to reveal the sword sheathed inside.

It seemed so long since April had seen this incarnation of Lord Petteril that she was stunned. This was the disreputable clerk, the apparent forger with the dangerous eyes blinking behind his spectacles who had first appeared in one of St. Giles's more lethal haunts, looking for her because he thought she'd stolen a necklace from him.

While Alf was still recovering from his shock, Lord Petteril let the sheath of the cane fall to the floor with a clatter and used the wickedly sharp blade to point to the bottle still grasped in Alf's hand.

"Put it down, if you'd be so good."

Alf obeyed before he meant to and then looked annoyed with himself. But since the sword point had followed him to the table, there wasn't a lot he could do. Except snatch his knife from his own pocket and glare at the newcomer.

"This ain't your patch, mister," Alf sneered. "Best back off now."

April held her breath, looking around wildly for a weapon of her own. Petteril, however, merely smiled—a bare stretch of his lips—as he gazed deliberately from the short knife to the length of his own sword.

"Oh, I think you'll catch cold at that, my friend. Time to—er... take yourself off," Petteril suggested.

"Scarper," April explained with some satisfaction. "Shab off."

"*You* don't employ me. He does." Alf jerked his head with contempt at Brandy Bill. "And he owes me."

"For what?" Bill growled. "You don't do your bleeding job. Got the lad to do it for you!"

"Forgive me," Petteril said politely to Alf. "How much are you owed?"

"Nothing," Bill interrupted with bitterness. "He's already helped hisself to my purse."

"Then perhaps we can agree to say no more about it," Petteril suggested. "Goodbye."

Alf opened his mouth, then glanced from the impudently grinning April to the hostile if badly weakened Bill, and finally to Petteril. Whatever he saw there must have convinced him that his game was over for he swore obscenely and stalked from the room. His boots clattered on the stairs.

Petteril's gaze finally met April's. His eyes were wintry, causing something to twist and shrivel inside her.

"Mrs. Gardner, please come in," he said without releasing April's gaze. It was she who looked away in surprise to see a plump, pretty woman a few years short of forty perhaps, who bustled into the room. April was at a loss to place her. She was no lady, but she did look very respectable.

"Mrs. Gardner once worked for my uncle, when I was a boy," Petteril explained. "She has come to look after..." He turned to the bed. "This gentleman."

"Here," Brandy Bill said nervously. "I been looked after enough for one day. Who the bleeding hell are you people and what are you all doing in my room?"

"You can cut out that kind of language for a start," Mrs. Gardner said tartly, marching up to the bed to stare at the hectic spots of colour on his greyish skin and take in the odd cloudiness of his eyes. "You've got a nasty fever. Is your wound infected?"

"It looks a bit red and puffy," April said, "but it ain't corrupted yet. I can't smell nothing."

"I've brought a dressing for it, and some tea to bring down the fever. But first, I think you need feeding up, Mr...?"

"Bill," said the highwayman warily.

"I brought you some soup. It's still warm so you can take it quickly."

While Bill looked as if he was in some kind of bad dream, and Mrs. Gardner searched the tiny cupboard for a bowl and spoon, April finally dared to look at Lord Petteril again.

He was retrieving the sheath of his sword stick, which slid home with a click.

"I didn't think you could find him," April blurted. "So I did it for you. Seems I was wrong."

"No. I didn't even look for him. I looked for you. And just as well I found you when I did."

"I'd have coped," April said, tilting her chin. "I always do."

The flash of anger in his uncharacteristically hard eyes was bad enough, but the fear she saw behind it defeated her utterly.

"I'd have got away," she muttered.

He stared at her. "Where to? You've nowhere to hide here. No friends or allies, just strangers in a strange, small place. Now we'll probably have to move Bill before your man comes back with his friends and we have to fight our way out with a gin bottle, a sword-stick and some lukewarm soup."

April emitted a sound that was half-snort, half-giggle. Lord Petteril spun away, but not before she'd caught the responsive twitch of his lips. Relief flooded her so hard it made her hands shake. His care still amazed her. Her own fear of losing that care scared her half to death.

Brandy Bill, by this time, was spooning thick, delicious-smelling broth into his mouth, while warily watching Mrs. Gardner.

Piers turned his gaze upon the highwayman and adjusted his spectacles, probably because his vision was blurry. April knew they were his reading glasses and he wore them only as part of this surprisingly effective disguise. It wasn't so much his appearance that was altered but his whole manner, his whole character.

"Let me begin," he said mildly to Bill, "by saying that I have neither the means nor the inclination to have you arrested for any crime that is not murder."

Bill eyed him uneasily. "You ain't the magistrate's clerk, are you?"

"No. My name is Withan."

"Bill," said Bill, with excessive caution considering everyone knew pretty exactly who and what he was. He frowned suddenly. "I knew a Captain Withan once. Decent officer. Died at Badajoz. The first siege."

Petteril's mask slipped. She had never seen the rawness of this specific grief before, and even now, taken by surprise, it vanished so quickly she might never have seen it.

"My cousin," he said.

"Sorry. I got hit at the same time, but I was luckier."

"Were you invalided out?"

"Aye. My leg never worked right after that." He grimaced. "Neither did I."

"So you took to the high toby? A friend of mine guessed that. Unexpectedly perceptive of him."

"If he's the cove that took my pistol and all but put me back on my horse, you'd better thank him for me. Could have laid me out for the magistrate and I'd be swinging by the end of the month." He swallowed another mouthful of soup. "Don't know why he didn't. Come to that, don't know why you don't neither. You all know I'm weak as a kitten."

"Thing is," Petteril said, "I want to know what you were doing in Petteril Wood last Monday night."

The highwayman's eyes grew wary again. "Camping out. Seemed like a good place to rest up while I healed. No one in the big house, no gamekeeper."

"Did you by chance see two gentleman in the wood that night?"

"No," Bill said. "But I saw a woman."

April sat down on the bottom of the bed, her eyes seeking Lord Petteril's.

He said slowly, "A woman? A woman stabbed Orr?" He frowned, shaking his head. "Maybe she was just dressed as a woman."

"Don't be daft," Bill scoffed, letting his spoon fall back into the bowl. "I can tell the difference."

"Can you?" Lord Petteril said without emphasis. He did not so much as glance at April. "Did you see who she was with? Can you describe her?"

"I never saw him, but I heard his voice. Talked like you, Mr. Withan. Or at least like you did when you first come in. Like a nob who ain't always been one." He looked Lord Petteril up and down with sudden interest. "You out of twig?"

"Definitely," Mrs. Gardner said with a sniff.

"Best round here," Bill said. "Stand out like a sore thumb otherwise."

"Indeed. Was she surprised to see this man?"

"Doubt it. She'd been waiting for him long enough and she was pleased enough to see him."

Petteril blinked. "How pleased? Remembering there is a lady present."

"Very pleased. All over him she was, and he didn't seem to mind. All over each other if you want the truth."

"Well," Petteril said. "It always bothered me that he took an overnight bag from the Dog and Duck, yet clearly meant to return to pack Hunter's things. I suppose an assignation explains it. Fellow wants to look his best. Even in the dark."

"Then they weren't quarrelling?" April said, frustrated.

"Wish they were. It would have been easier to creep away. Which I still managed to do without them hearing or seeing."

"What did you do then?" Petteril asked. "Just go back to your camp?"

"To get my horse and my pack. Skirted around them and rode on to Blanchester." He flexed the arm on his injured side. "Didn't do me wound much good but the woods were suddenly too busy for me."

"Did you see either of them again? Hear them?" Petteril asked.

"A bit."

"Quarrels? Screams?"

"Nah. Just voices, muffled by the trees." He frowned. "I smelled a fresh fire, though, from the road. Could make out the glow, but that was all. More interested in keeping out of their way."

April could understand that, though it was damned annoying. They so nearly had a witness to the whole thing. Though, of course, Brandy Bill could hardly give evidence without admitting who he was to the authorities who would be obliged to hang him for highway robbery. Mr. Alleyn, Lord Maxwell, and Laura Lindon would probably all recognize his voice, even if his face had been masked.

"What about the woman?" Lord Petteril asked at last. "Did you know her?"

"Nah, 'course not."

"Then you'd never seen her before? Or since?"

Bill grinned. "No, and trust me, I'd remember."

Not Laura Lindon, then...

Lord Petteril asked hastily, "Was she a lady or someone of a lower order?"

"Oh, definitely a lady."

"Young or old? Fat or thin? Dark or fair? What was she wearing?"

"Mr. Piers, don't harass the man," Mrs. Gardner scolded. "He's ill and doing his best."

"Only 'cause you're Captain Withan's brother," Bill said with sudden ferocity. "I thought she were young at first, and she were a handsome piece, dark hair, slender like a girl. But she moved wrong, like a much more mature lady, you know? And when the man lifted the lantern high, I could see the lines on her face and neck."

Involuntarily, it seemed, Lord Petteril looked at April.

"Mrs. Lindon," she said huskily.

"*Mrs. Lindon flirts with everyone,*" Piers murmured, quoting from an earlier conversation with April. Removing his spectacles to rub his eyes felt like throwing off the filters of childhood. The woman *did* flirt with him, with her guests, even those she despised socially, like Alleyn. As though she were searching for something she never found. A beautiful, discontented woman, no longer young.

The enormity of the possibilities cut through the remains of his worry for April, forcing him to think rather than feel, and there was relief in that.

April, none the worse for her adventures, said to the highwayman, "Could the man with her in the wood have been Lord Maxwell? The man you held up?"

"Could have been. I didn't see his face. Didn't sound much like him. But the woman weren't the girl in that gig."

"Are you sure?" Piers asked. "They look quite alike, especially from a distance."

"The girl in the gig was young," Bill insisted.

"Let him rest now," Mrs. Gardner said, taking his bowl away and offering him a sip of ale.

Frowning in distraction, Piers felt he was hovering on the edge of some vital truth. He moved away from the bed to the window. April followed him.

"Would she really have an affair with her daughter's betrothed?" Piers wondered aloud. "Could that have been the real reason she supported the match? To make being with him easier?"

"Then where does Orr fit in?" April asked. "He saw them together so they had to kill him?"

Piers shook his head, more in annoyance than disagreement. "But what was Orr doing there in the first place? Following his master for purposes of blackmail? It doesn't feel right."

"It ain't right," April agreed. "Don't stop it being true."

"It *jangles*," Piers said, rubbing the side of his hand along his forehead. "In my brain. It doesn't feel right. Not for Mrs. Lindon and not for Hunter. He's an unmitigated rake but he has his own code of honour. Even for money he would never have agreed to marry his mistress's daughter. And Mrs. Lindon...I just can't see her doing anything so sordid."

April shrugged. Very little about human behaviour surprised her. "You don't really know either of 'em."

He sighed, leaning back against the window sill. "True. But we're missing something. And we have no evidence except the word of a highwayman that she was even in the woods that night."

"He wouldn't admit it to the law, either. They'd just say he was in the right place and he did it. They'd hang him anyway."

Mrs. Gardner came over to them, frowning. "Is this man safe here?"

"No," Piers said, straightening. "No, he isn't. We could take him to the Dog and Duck, pretend he's some old coachman of my father's."

"Or he could stay at my cottage where I can more easily nurse him back to health."

"You think he'll live?" April asked her.

"He hasn't got the look of a dead man. Just a sick and hopeless one. I can say he's my cousin who used to work for your father, Mr. Piers, and then went to America."

Piers looked at her, frowning. "He's a highwayman, Mrs, G. He's Brandy Bill."

"So I gathered," she said. The faintest of flushes seemed to seep into her face. "But he's not exactly dangerous, is he?"

"Not away from the public highway. But you'd be harbouring a fugitive."

"Are *you* going to tell Mr. Lindon?"

Piers considered. "No. I'm going to hope the subject doesn't come up and bring you some clothes for him."

"I have Mr. Gardner's clothes still. I can alter them."

Piers smiled at her. He was glad he had thought to call in and ask for her help. "The question is, can he walk to the inn?"

It seemed he could—just—supported by Piers and Mrs. Gardner, while April acted as guard. She carried the sword stick and twirled it threateningly toward anyone who looked too curious. Once they reached the more respectable part of town, she merely trailed after them like a good servant.

Piers, who had already found the pony and gig used by his kitchen staff, directed April to drive it and follow him with Mrs. Gardner, while he took Brandy Bill in his curricle.

Exhausted by his efforts, the highwayman seemed to be asleep for most of the way. "Who's she then?" he asked once, and Piers, following his own train of thought, assumed for a moment he meant April.

Fortunately, he pulled himself up in time. "Mrs. Gardner worked for my family from when she was a child until she married Mr. Gardner. She is now a widow, and entitled to every respect which, despite your recent occupation, I am trusting you to accord to her. For her own sake and my cousin's."

Bill regarded him with displeasure, then his head fell back. "Got to say that, don't you? I wouldn't hurt a hair on her head, even without your warnings. Even if she never met Captain Withan. But I'm a wanted man, sir. I shouldn't be staying in her house."

"That's between you and Mrs. Gardner," he said.

Bill opened his eyes and grinned tiredly, "Meaning you couldn't influence her if you tried."

"Meaning exactly that," Piers agreed.

There was no further conversation until they arrived at Mrs. Gardner's cottage a few miles outside the town. Bill was duly settled in the spare room with and being threatened with a wash and a clean nightgown when Piers and April slipped out, grinning.

By now, without protest, April was back in her blue dress and white cap, her boy's clothes stashed in the carpet bag. Since it was growing dark, Piers insisted they left the pony cropping grass in the paddock behind the cottage and took April up in the curricle.

She was silent for the first five minutes of the journey back. Then she said, "What should we do now?"

"Persuade everyone to tell the truth," Piers said ruefully. "Which is not going to be easy."

"What do you think happened to Orr?"

"I think... I think he was having an affair with Mrs. Lindon. Probably, they encountered each other at the same house party where Laura first met Hunter. He would be attractive, forbidden fruit to her. Not just adultery, but with a man not of her class."

"And *she* stabbed him? Why'd she do that, then?"

"I don't know. Some betrayal we know nothing of. It would explain her burning his clothes in rage."

"Would it?" April said doubtfully. "And then creeping around to burn the boots in the Alleyns' fire?" She straightened. "We never found his bag, did we? Either she must have got rid of it already or she's biding her time. Where'd a lady stash something like that so it stayed hidden?"

"In her own rooms, I suppose. Though even there, surely her maid could come across it."

"We need to search her rooms, then."

Piers shuddered. "What, shall we get Lindon to issue a warrant?"

April blinked at him. "Don't be daft. I'll find a way."

"No breaking in," Piers said severely. "We must find another solution."

"Tell her poor husband to help us find proof she were having an affair with a servant?" April scoffed.

Piers sighed. "One way or another, he'll have to know." How ever this turned out, Lindon was likely to be embarrassed at the very least, and very probably unbearably hurt and humiliated.

"Not if she didn't do it," April argued. "None of it needs to come out unless she was the one who killed Orr." The carriage light on the side of the curricle showed her thoughtful, concentrated expression. It was a fascinating face in many ways, so young and yet so full of character. A child who had seen and suffered too much. She wasn't untouched by that. She merely moved beyond it.

"When's this ball at Lindon Grange?" she asked.

"Tomorrow night."

"Why don't you offer your own servants' help? Then I can spin a yarn about my ambition to become a lady's maid one day and in a quiet moment, get Mrs. Lindon's woman to show me her rooms and what she does there."

Piers raised his eyebrows with considerable respect. "That is actually quite clever. Mrs. Lindon herself is unlikely to go there during the ball. Only, you can't exactly poke about in the closets and crawl under the bed with her maid watching you."

"No, I need to get rid of her somehow," April agreed. "Perhaps you could help there."

"Perhaps I could."

Chapter Twelve

On the day of the ball, Laura Lindon was surprised to return from a morning ride to be summoned to her mother's boudoir. She was even more surprised to find her father and brother also present.

"We want to warn you," Oscar said, almost as soon as Laura came in and shut the door, "that we no longer think it advisable to announce your betrothal this evening."

Laura paused, then walked forward and sat down in the vacant chair. "Good. Because Lord Maxwell and I do not wish to be married." It was true, but for some reason, she felt no relief let alone joy in her unexpected release.

Her father cast his eyes to heaven. "Since when?"

Laura shrugged. "I cannot speak for him. But for me, since you first told me I was engaged to marry him."

"She is obedient," Mama said with a trace of regret. "She will marry where you tell her."

Papa scowled. "As I recall, it was you and Oscar who thought Maxwell Hunter such a fine idea. I always had my doubts, but Oscar moves more in society than I do."

"We want to manage this in a civilized manner," Oscar said to Laura. "We don't want the Hunters taking a pet when you become engaged to Petteril instead."

"Petteril?" she repeated, startled. "You want me to jilt Maxwell for Piers?"

"You've known him all your life," her father said as though reciting a lesson. "He is considerably cleverer and much more financially stable than Maxwell, and Oscar thinks he may well be the up and coming man—in terms of wealth and politics."

Laura forced herself to think through her dismay. She was not free, she was just in bondage to someone else. Was Piers any better? She liked him well enough. He had that quirky sense of humour so that when he said something one was never quite sure whether or not he was joking. He was innately kind, and knowledgeable, and his eyes laughed.

Maxwell's eyes laughed too. If she was honest, she rather liked them, and since he had released her from her engagement, the quality of the tension she felt around him had changed. She didn't know what that meant either. She just knew she didn't want to be pushed from man to man like a decanter of after-dinner port.

She said, "Piers has no reason to marry me."

"Then give him one," Oscar said succinctly. "Tonight would be a good time to begin. So the world will not imagine for a moment that Maxwell found you wanting, only that you prefer Petteril."

"And therefore find Maxwell wanting?"

"Don't be awkward," Oscar said irritably. "Hunter will take it well enough."

"I doubt Petteril will," Laura said. "I doubt he is as easily pushed around as you seem to imagine."

Oscar laughed. "Now there you are wrong. I know Piers a great deal better than you do. He has grown up rather well, but people do not change."

Somehow Laura got out of the room without losing her temper. But inside, she burned with fury and with something else she could not name.

She did not get the chance to speak to Lord Maxwell about it until the family and house guests began to gather in the ballroom that evening. She had not been placed beside him at the light, pre-ball dinner, which she had found so annoying that she had tried to glare at her mother for altering the seating arrangement. Only, Mama had looked so distracted, so...vulnerable that Laura had been concerned instead of angry. Maxwell had asked once if her mother were ill. For the first time, Laura began to wonder.

As she entered the ballroom, Maxwell was only one of several who came to meet her, exclaiming over the beauty of her person and her gown. Once, it would have mattered a great deal to her. Tonight, she smiled with polite gratitude, but she found she did not really care. As soon as she civilly could, she took Maxwell's arm and hauled him off to inspect the potted plants that decorated the ballroom. He submitted with amused good nature.

"Has my father spoken to you?" she asked abruptly.

"About what?" he asked, eyeing the slightly wilted palm with some doubt.

"Our marriage."

"No. I thought he came to speak to me after dinner, but he didn't say anything."

"He's probably ashamed," Laura said intensely. "And so he should be. He's decided I shouldn't marry you after all."

Maxwell's lashes fanned over his cheek as he glanced at the floor. Then he looked up at her again, his expression amiable if slightly surprised. "That is what you wanted. Aren't you happy?"

"Are you?" she countered after the smallest pause.

"I am glad they are paying attention to your wishes at last."

"But they aren't! They want me to marry Lord Petteril instead!"

Maxwell's breath caught, but his expression did not change. "Decent fellow, Petteril. I rather like him. Different, but probably fun on a spree."

A flush of annoyance washed over her. "I doubt he will take his wife on many sprees!"

"He might. I'd take mine."

"Would you?" she asked, distracted in spite of herself.

"Depending on the company, of course, but I'd like my wife to be friends with my friends. Or at least some of them."

She could not help the giggle that escaped. "So long as you do not introduce her to your other women!"

"Oh, I'd have no other women if I was married," he said carelessly, and for some reason a glow settled around her heart.

"Wouldn't you?" she said, smiling.

He smiled back and shook his head, and suddenly everything in her was melting. Happily melting.

"Laura!" came her mother's unusually sharp voice. "Our guests are arriving!"

"I must go," she said, curiously breathless as she detached her hand from his arm. As she hurried over to her mother's side, she had the odd sensation she was floating. She smiled quite genuinely at all the friends and neighbours who arrived, including the Alleyns, and Lord Petteril. She had almost forgotten her parents' wishes for him.

"How delightful to see you this evening!" her mother greeted him. "Laura in particular has been so looking forward to dancing with you."

Laura felt her face burn with embarrassment, especially since Petteril's rather haughty eyebrows flew up. He had never been haughty as a boy, she was sure.

"With me?" he exclaimed. "But you must know I don't dance. I warn every ball hostess that I am a waste of their space."

Mama's expression was almost ludicrous. Laura wanted to giggle, and Lord Petteril met her gaze with humour dancing in his eyes. "Perhaps I can explain my affliction to you instead?" he said. "If you have nothing better to do, of course, which I find very unlikely!"

Laura laughed and turned to the vicar instead. She did like Petteril. He was funny and intriguing and just as different as Maxwell had said. But she didn't imagine she would ever understand him, and it came to her quite clearly that she did not want to marry him.

She wanted to marry Lord Maxwell.

PIERS WAS NOT BLIND to the little scene played out as he was received. Mrs. Lindon's welcome was subtly different. She no longer flirt-
ed as she directed him to her daughter. Which he found interesting.
Had the Lindons changed horses, as it were, and now in pursuit of *him*?

A frightening ambition, but not one he was prepared to indulge, as
much for Laura's sake as his own. Even supposing her mother had not
committed murder, and that seemed very unlikely. He believed Brandy
Bill's description. She had been the one Orr had come to the woods to
meet, as soon as his master had given him leave.

She would hardly be the first slighted or betrayed lover to kill. And
it was true there was a certain weariness about her movements. It struck
him that he had never noticed she was flirting with him because she
hadn't actually meant it. It was automatic with her, simply how she
communicated with men, only the spark had gone out of it. Surely,
there was a subtle difference in her from when he had first met her
again? As though the weight of her crime was pressing gradually upon
her shoulders and her conscience, slowly destroying her...

He stopped as someone spoke to him and glanced back at her, now
welcoming the Alleyns to the ball, and that sense of wrongness shuddered through him. He had known her most of his life in a very distant
kind of a way. It was hard to see her as a killer.

And he would have to keep his wits about him if he was to be any
help to April's search. Even that made him feel grubby and ashamed,
like an over-curious schoolboy. The effect of her crime on her family
was going to be devastating, and yet he could not keep this quiet, could
not look away. A man had *died*. And life, however painful, was pre-
cious. No one was more aware of that than Piers.

The trio of hired musicians in the corner struck up and the ball
opened with Mrs. Lindon partnering Lord Maxwell—since she had
been deprived of Piers, the highest ranking of her guests, by his "affliction". His affliction, of course, was his inability to remember or rec-

ognize faces, which made a social nightmare out of trying to find the ladies whom one had earlier invited to dance. It was much simpler not to dance at all. And the creation of his haughty viscount role allowed him to stroll among the other guests, glass in hand, distantly nodding to anyone who caught his eye.

"Ah, my lord Petteril!" an elderly gentleman greeted him with great affability, thrusting out his hand. "Pleasure to meet you at last! Haven't seen you since you were a lad running wild with the old viscount's boys, what?"

"How do you do, sir?" Piers said, shaking hands and wondering who the devil this was. Eventually, from the topic of discussion, he worked out that he was a more distant neighbour whose land touched Haybury at an apparently vital point currently being taken advantage of by his lordship's steward.

Piers, his eye caught by Laura dancing with one of the young men who might have attended his garden party, agreed to look into the matter at the first opportunity. He walked with the elderly gentleman towards the wine, passed him a glass and toasted old friendship before abandoning him to a middle aged lady and turning to find Oscar Lindon beside him.

"I was sorry not to see you open the ball with my mother," Oscar said, after the first greeting. "Perhaps you are not aware of the custom, having spent so long in academic life."

"Oh, I couldn't. I explained it to your mother when I arrived. She is most understanding and truly her dignity was much safer with Hunter." He gave Oscar a small smile. "There is no insult. I never dance."

Oscar gazed at him, almost uncomprehending. "Never? Don't you find that awkward? It is *expected*."

"One doesn't always have to do the expected." Piers said vaguely. Already he felt Oscar's pain when his mother's crime was revealed. Probably, it would be the end of his own political and social ambitions.

And Laura's marriage. The Hunters would reject her, and her chances would be ruined. Lindon himself would be devastated.

So much simpler to keep quiet, sweep it all under the carpet, and let life go on. Surely Mrs. Lindon would never kill again...? This had to be a crime of passion.

"Perhaps you have that luxury," Oscar said, with the veriest hint of envy. "We lesser mortals must follow the rules for the sake of our families and our futures. We cannot step outside those invisible boundaries of custom, propriety, and taste. Not if we are to maintain our position in society, let alone improve it."

"You are probably right," Piers said peaceably. "I am conscious of my own privilege —and my own selfishness. But you are not dancing yourself."

"I will be. Don't you find balls dull if you never dance?"

"No. I catch the young ladies exhausted by too much exercise and gain their favour by finding them a place to rest and drink lemonade. They are much too grateful for the respite to be bored."

Oscar looked amused. "An interesting strategy. I might try it some time. Do you have any particular lady in your sights? Do you think of marriage?"

"No," Piers said uncompromisingly. He raised his glass. "Good luck," he murmured and strolled on toward Mrs. Alleyn who was sitting by herself just a few yards away. She was quite a distinctive figure in her over-flounced gown and too many jewels. And with too few companions. No one forgave the nouveau riches, the vulgar people in trade who thought money could buy them acceptance into the upper echelons of society. Even here in the country, where the echelons were not so high. Except his own, of course.

Something was nagging at him, the feeling that he did not know his neighbours well enough, the knowledge that he did not understand the murder of Nathaniel Orr—surely another ambitious young man with tastes above his station in life. Like Oscar, in his own way. Or Samuel Alleyn.

"Good evening, Mrs. Alleyn." He bowed and the lady looked up with surprise.

"My lord! Good evening." She looked even more surprised when he sat down beside her.

Piers was not a great man for small talk, but he made the effort and discovered her interests lay primarily in her family, her house and her garden. He had the impression she was lonely, but as much from the frequent absence of her husband and son as from the snobbery of her neighbours which she accepted as part of life.

"I'm very grateful to be invited, as I'm sure you understand, my lord. Mostly for Sam's sake, to be honest. His father and me stepped up out of our place but he was brought up to be a gentleman and it goes hard with him to be looked down on by lesser men."

"And women?" he asked gently, following her gaze to Samuel, who stood among some other young people and yet seemed somehow apart from the group. His gaze was on Laura Lindon, laughing up at her dancing partner. She looked very beautiful, almost glowing with enjoyment.

Mrs. Alleyn sighed. "I've told him that won't wash. Laura is a lovely young lady. No haughtiness in her. But the Lindons would never have my Sam."

"Does he mind a great deal?"

"I think he had hope before Lord Maxwell came. It will be easier for him when they tie the knot and she moves away from here. But he's a boy of strong feeling, my Sam. He's taking it badly."

"The love or the...condescension for want of a better word?"

"Both," she said ruefully. "His father says he has no ambition, but he does. It's just different from his. But you don't want to hear about my family troubles! How are you settling in to Haybury Court?"

He stayed chatting for another minute or two, by which time the next dance set was forming and he saw Laura's hand claimed by Lord Maxwell. Her smile jolted Piers, for it was no longer indifferent. Not remotely. Another tragedy to be caused by the revelation of her mother's guilt.

She danced with Samuel after that. There was something proprietorial in his manner that gave Piers pause. Whether it was love or ambition or a heady combination of the two, Mrs. Alleyn was right. He was not giving up on Laura easily. Could *he* have been the one to kill Orr after all? Mistaking Mrs. Lindon for Laura? And Orr for Lord Maxwell, whom he had not then met. In some ways, it would be an easier solution, at least for the Lindons. Not for the Alleyns. And if Samuel's motives came out in the trial, then the Lindons would be ruined anyway.

For a moment, Piers wished he had left the matter alone. Without him, Lindon would never have found the truth and everything would stay the same. But the truth had to matter.

Deliberately, he put himself in Laura's way as the dance ended, presenting her with a glass of wine and bearing her off to a corner seat. He had been going to try to talk to her gently about her mother, perhaps discover if he could how Evangela's affair with Orr began and who in her family might possibly be aware of her infidelity, or her grief at his death.

But Laura took him by surprise. "I'm very glad to talk with you, Piers. I need to warn you that my parents now favour you over Lord Maxwell. I know you won't be as easy to manoeuvre as they imagine, but you should be warned! Don't be alarmed, however, I have not agreed to it and I won't."

Piers closed his mouth, unable to think what to say. "Thank you," he murmured at last, and she laughed.

"You would be such a fun husband. I'm almost sorry neither of us wants it."

Guilt settled in his stomach like a stone. When the truth came out, Maxwell would flee. Even if he didn't wish to, his family would insist. He tried to be dispassionate, to see her in terms of his other theory, that it really had been Laura with Orr, not her mother, whatever Brandy Bill thought he saw. Women could pretend so much more easily than men...

No, that was not true. Women could more easily pull the wool over *Piers's* eyes because he had had less to do with them. His university friends, associates and students had all been men. He might not have recognized all their faces all the time, but he could read their expressions like a book and knew exactly when they lied and why. Women were a much more exotic breed—delightful, pleasurable, but incomprehensible.

Laura could probably fool him very easily. He tried to imagine her with Orr, killing him perhaps to keep him from telling Maxwell of their affair. Her innocence, the gentle unfurling of her love for Maxwell, could all be faked. She *could* be that cold-hearted.

But he really didn't think so. Neither, more to the point, did April. Very few people of any class pulled the wool over her eyes.

As though his thought conjured a reaction, one of the Lindon footmen materialized beside him and bent to murmur in his ears. "April wanted your lordship to know she is still here at the Grange, and to send to her for any requirement."

Which meant that April, who had come over much earlier in the day to help the Lindon staff prepare for the ball, had succeeded in her plan so far, and was on her way to view Mrs. Lindon's rooms. Which at least gave him a positive task.

"Thank you," Piers said mildly. "I'm glad she is of help."

MISS JONES WAS MRS. Lindon's personal maid. Although merely a local girl, she had become so used to lording it over most other servants in the neighbourhood that she had developed a regal and self-satisfied air. With a mixture of awe, respect, and persistence, April had found it relatively easy to get Miss Jones to explain her work and show her the mistress's rooms.

April was even pleased with the way she pretended a hint of guilt when she asked a harassed footman to explain her continued presence to his lordship. Her only worry was that the footman might forget, which would probably make all her effort count for nothing. Without her word, Lord Petteril would not know when she needed rid of Miss Jones.

April's awe at Mrs. Lindon's exquisitely feminine bedchamber and sitting room was very real. There was a certain luxury about the bed and its beautiful hangings, and the chaise longue with its many cushions, that reminded her of the brothel upstairs at the Queen's Head. Except that here the colours blended rather than clashed. The window curtains matched those of the bed, and everything was muted by good taste. In fact, the rooms were rather lovely and she did not need to pretend her admiration.

She listened avidly to Miss Jones's descriptions of her duties and how to care for the beautiful clothes she was allowed to touch with her clean fingertips. She sniffed the perfumes and oils with delight and gasped at the sparkling jewels.

Mrs. Lindon, she reflected, did pretty well for a squire's wife. Not that April was an expert in the different ranks and wealth of the nobs, but she did know the Petteril house and estate was much bigger, and she had seen his lordship's aunt and cousins dressed up for London balls. Mrs. Lindon would not have looked out of place. Although perhaps her gowns were fewer, and possibly older. April could not tell the difference between last season's fashions and this, but she knew they existed.

Every door, every drawer that was opened, she peered into, hoping for a glimpse of a bag out of place that might conceivably have belonged to Orr. But, of course, Mrs. Lindon would never have put it where her maid was likely to discover it. So April touched and surreptitiously pulled at drawers to see if they were locked.

They were not, apart, she expected from the roll-top desk, which Miss Jones touched but did not open as she explained that she was also responsible for ensuring writing materials were always available there.

"It must be very hard work, so much to remember," April said doubtfully. "I'm not sure I could do it... Unless I had a very understanding mistress! Is Mrs. Lindon forgiving?"

Miss Jones sniffed. "She does not have to be. I know my duties." Then she relented. "I didn't always, of course. Everyone has to learn, and Mrs. Lindon being sharp certainly made me learn quickly. I'm sure in time you'll be as good as me."

"Do you like her?" April asked, gazing up at the cornice of the sitting room.

"Not our place to like or dislike," Miss Jones said sternly.

By which April understood that she did not. A quick glance showed her faintly pursed lips, a hint of distaste in the eyes, quickly banished. *She disapproves of her.* Which meant Miss Jones was not entirely ignorant of what her mistress got up to.

"Of course, she is so beautiful," April said. "Especially for a more mature lady. She must have lots of admirers."

"Has them eating out of her hand," Miss Jones said with a pride somewhat at odds with her distaste. "Of course, I always send her out so perfectly dressed and groomed..."

"Miss Jones?" a footman called from just outside the door to the passage. "Are you in there? Mistress wants you!"

April, torn between excitement and frustration—she had the feeling Miss Jones had been on the verge of some confidence—stayed where she was as the maid hurried to the door.

"What is it?" she demanded.

"She says you've to take the pearl-headed hair pins and wait for her in the blue reception room."

The footman's steps rushed away again, leaving April to understand the message was really from Lord Petteril, telling April to meet him in the blue reception room with whatever she discovered, once Miss Jones had abandoned it.

Miss Jones bolted to the bedchamber. "You see?" she called over her shoulder to April. "Never a moment to yourself! Always on duty!"

"Worth it though," April said from the sitting room, maintaining the awe in her voice.

Miss Jones rushed past, stuffing pins into her apron pocket. "Wait there, don't touch. I won't be long..."

She left the door open, and April didn't dare to close it. Instead, she strode past it, hastily opening all the drawers she hadn't managed to test before. She looked in the cupboard of the bedside table, which was not locked, and under the bed where she found only an elegant porcelain chamber pot.

She opened the cupboard of the nightstand, stood on a chair to feel the top of the wardrobe and looked inside the small portmanteau she discovered there. Nothing. And she could be running out of time.

She put the chair back where she had found it, and hastened through to the sitting room. The roll top desk was indeed locked. April opened the flap of the leather bag at her belt and felt inside for the little spikes that any self-respecting dub prig would recognize. The lock was easy to pick.

She dropped the spiky tool back in her bag and, holding her breath, she rolled back the top. Paper, ink, pens, sand. No bag. And the drawers below were too small to contain anything more than sealing wax.

Nothing. *Bugger and damnation.*

"What are you doing there?"

April literally jumped and spun around to see Oscar Lindon glaring at her from the doorway.

Chapter Thirteen

Laura was delighted to walk out onto the terrace with Lord Maxwell. Her father watched her go, unease in his face. But he did not interfere. Perhaps he thought she was about to give Maxwell his congé.

There was not much moon, but her mother had extravagantly placed lanterns all along the paths of the formal garden. Another couple strolling in front of Laura and Maxwell, turned into the right hand path. Blossom petals softened the ground beneath her dancing slippers, and the smell of spring flowers and freshly cut grass scented the air.

Laura's heart beat like a drum. She had no idea what to say, how to be sure... Almost desperately, she said, "Isn't it odd how we have become friends?"

"Whatever else, I shall never regret that."

She turned her head to see him better. "Do you regret...other things?"

"Many things," he said ruefully. "I came here, to you, a blatant fortune hunter, so selfish that I never even considered you. Being such a fine and handsome fellow, I took your agreement for granted."

"My parents will have fostered that belief."

He drew in his breath. "I have nothing, Laura, but a tarnished reputation, a string of scandals and debts. Everyone knows my pockets are to let. But I do have a tidy little property in Suffolk that could be made to work to support a wife and family, if we spent most of the year there. It's not much to offer in return for a lady defying her family."

Her heart seemed to be beating now in her throat. "It might be," she managed. "In certain circumstances."

He flung back his head, staring upward at the sky as though searching for inspiration. "You could have everything with Petteril. With almost anyone else. Men will fall over themselves to offer for you. All I have is love, and I don't even know what to do with that because I've never really loved a woman before. It all depends on whether you are happier with or without me. Please speak quickly and put me out of my misery."

In growing wonder, she gazed at his upturned face. The smile forming on her lips seemed to be quite out of her control.

"With you," she whispered.

He straightened his head slowly until he met her gaze. "Really?" he said unsteadily.

She only nodded, and stepped closer, turning her face up to his. Only then did his arms come around her and he lowered his head to kiss her.

His mouth fitted perfectly over hers, softly parting her lips, which clung to his as sweetness and wonder overwhelmed her. She was loved.

PIERS'S NAGGING SENSE of impending disaster did not fade, even when he had sent the footman with the false message for Mrs. Lindon's maid. If April found Orr's bag, Mrs. Lindon was unquestionably guilty, with all the horrific implications for her family. If she didn't find it, it proved nothing, except that she had got rid of it. Which would be best for the Lindons.

But what of Orr's family? Those shadowy, unknown people to whom his body was being returned so that they might grieve and mourn in the usual way. Piers could not wish that on anyone, friend or stranger.

In his heart, Piers believed Brandy Bill's description. The woman with Orr could only have been Mrs. Lindon. So why did the solution feel so wrong? Because there was more to learn?

Piers slipped out of the ballroom and walked past the blue reception room, where a frowning maid was pacing the floor. She looked eagerly toward the door as he passed, and then continued pacing. Guiltily, Piers strode on to the next room and threw himself into a chair to think.

Did the solution to the murder feel wrong because it was not the full solution? Was there something about Mrs. Lindon he did not know?

Many things.

But he was rarely wrong about basics. He might not know or understand Mrs. Lindon very well, but he did not sense ungovernable rage or evil in her. Merely discontent, which was a little tame to inspire murder and the burning of her victim's clothes.

Was it possible Mrs. Lindon had been with Orr but not killed him? That, he could imagine much more easily, but someone had most definitely murdered the valet. If not her, then who?

Someone who had seen them together. The betrayed Mr. Lindon, in defence of his own and his wife's honour? Oscar or even Laura in defence of their mother's?

Or had someone less perceptive in the darkness than Brandy Bill, mistaken the mother for the daughter? Could Samuel Alleyn have seen Orr with someone he thought was Laura and attacked him? There was enough anger in Samuel, and all the ruthlessness of his father. And he could most easily have put Orr's boots in the garden fire.

"*I think he had hope before Lord Maxwell came,*" his mother had said. "*He is a boy of strong feeling, my Sam. He's taking it badly.*"

Piers's mind jumped to Lindon, father of the girl who inspired such emotion. Lindon, the country squire and upstanding magistrate, quite out of his depth dealing with murder. Because he had committed that murder and was torn apart by that as much as by wife's adultery? If so, would he really have come straight to Piers to tell him about it and welcome his help? To welcome a prospective son-in-law with a murder inquiry was surely not his choice. The whole point of the Hunter alliance had been to connect with the powerful aristocracy. Not something Lindon seemed to care about much. He liked being a big fish in this small, country pond, though it was probably not enough for his bored wife or his ambitious son. His ambitious and slightly unstable son. Did Oscar really think he could brush off Hunter and acquire Petteril so easily? Knowing nothing about him since his boyhood?

The child is father of the man, according to a poem he had once read. With a twist of his stomach, he acknowledged that Oscar was the one of his suspects he really did know. Consciously or otherwise, he had been pushing their shared boyhood out of his mind, because it was uncomfortable, because Oscar had witnessed the way Piers's cousins and brother had turned on him. The old betrayal that no longer mattered.

It was Oscar, not Ivor, who had pulled Piers out of the river while the others laughed at his clumsiness. Oscar, furious at getting his clothes wet, and brave enough to do what he saw had to be done. Other memories flashed before him: Oscar, laughing with delight as he soared through the air on the swing they had rigged up between trees; Oscar, shoving Ivor to the ground in rage because he had said something derogatory about his family. What was it Ivor had said? Nothing, he had merely imitated Mrs. Lindon's walk, the seductive swaying of her hips and they had all laughed until Oscar's anger made them ashamed.

Piers' breath caught, as he hovered on the cusp of some vital understanding. And abruptly, Oscar's words tonight echoed in his head. *"We lesser mortals must follow the rules for the sake of our families and our futures. We cannot step outside those invisible boundaries of custom, propriety, and taste. Not if we are to maintain our position in society, let alone improve it."*

Piers jumped to his feet. *Boundaries of custom, propriety, and taste...*

Propriety and taste...

Ivor had crossed that boundary as a boy. But Oscar... As a man, Oscar had seen his mother with the valet. Perhaps he had even followed her, suspecting her of an assignation and meaning to put a stop to it before Lord Maxwell arrived to celebrate his betrothal to Laura. Oscar had been at the same winter party. He probably recognized the valet and knew damned well it was not Lord Maxwell. Surely that lapse in taste, the vulgarity not only of taking a lover but of taking a *servant* for her lover, had driven him to fury. To murder. To burning Orr's clothes. And boots. But possibly not the bag.

If that still existed, it would be in Oscar's rooms, not Mrs. Lindon's.

Without conscious thought he was striding back into the ballroom, his quizzing glass to his eye as he searched for Oscar. He wasn't very clear whether he meant to approach him now or assure himself he was in the ballroom before barging upstairs to search the man's rooms. This was beyond a quiet word with his father...

This was truth. He felt it in his bones. Oscar had gone away immediately after the murder, probably to recover his composure, or even to avoid having to identify the body. To Piers's knowledge, Oscar had never told anyone where he had been. No one had asked. Not even Piers himself.

Oscar was not in the ballroom, nor in the card room off it. In the garden? Possibly.

His stomach twisted painfully. April was alone upstairs, without Mrs. Lindon's maid. And he didn't know where Oscar was. Trying not to draw attention to himself in his haste, he sauntered out of the ballroom once more, then bolted for the back stairs and took them three at a time.

He almost burst into the passage above and had to jerk back again as Oscar himself came out of the first door on his left. Piers waited in an agony of indecision. He didn't know which room was Mrs. Lindon's, but surely Oscar would not go in there. He was going toward the main stairs at the end of the passage. And since he had left his own door open, Piers darted in and began to search.

APRIL GAZED WARILY at Oscar Lindon.

"Doing?" she said. "Nothing. Just waiting for Miss Jones. She's showing me how to become a lady's maid."

"Where is Jones?"

"Mrs. Lindon sent for her, but she'll be right back."

Oscar's frown vanished, then reformed into a positive scowl. He stepped forward. "Wait, you're that odd girl of Petteril's."

"Assistant," April said.

His lip curled with contempt and she blushed furiously at the thoughts she knew were going through his head. "Well, you'll have to go before his betrothal."

She stared at him. "I ain't planning to stay here for months on end. Your mam wouldn't like it and I got things to do."

"Well, go and do them. I don't know what Jones is thinking about to bring you up here, let alone leave you unattended."

April, with nothing more to look for, was quite happy to go. She was almost past him when his hand shot out and closed around her arm. She acted instinctively as she always did in such situations, jerking away so quickly and with such force that she took him by surprise. The sleeve of her dress tore, much to her fury, but he was glaring beyond her at the open desk.

Damn. She hadn't had time to close it, let alone click the lock back in place.

"Were you poking among my mother's things? Stealing? Reading her letters?"

"Don't be daft," April said brashly. "I ain't no thief, and I can barely read, neither."

"Then why are you always scribbling in that damned book?" He stared at the bag at her waist. "What did you take? Empty that bag at your belt."

"I will not," April said stoutly, though she didn't care for the rage which had suddenly appeared in his eyes. Why? Because he thought she'd prigged his mother's jewels? No, the anger had truly ignited *after* he had accused her of stealing. When he had said, *"Reading her letters?"*

That was what he feared. Because she might have read something proving his mother's affair. Which meant Oscar himself knew.

The air seemed to vanish from her lungs. Oscar knew. Had he seen his mother with Orr? Had *he* killed the valet?

She blinked, staring at the muzzle of a small, silver-handled pistol, pointing straight at her heart.

"Empty the bag," he ordered. "Now."

Slowly, she opened it, drew out the book, the pencil, the handkerchief containing her little dubman's tools. She tensed as he snatched them from her, then threw them on the floor and actually reached into the bag. She was afraid to move in case he shot her.

Grunting, he took his hand away but didn't step back let alone lower the pistol. "Read them already? Did they make you laugh? Give you something salacious to giggle over with Petteril? Well that is not going to happen. Petteril is never going to know because he's going to marry my sister. I'd give you the choice of leaving him or dying. Only I don't trust you to go."

April poised to charge him. She had nothing to lose now, and she so wanted to live this amazing new life she had found with *him*...

"Don't pull that trigger, Oscar," his voice said from the doorway, just as if she'd conjured him from her thoughts. "That would be murder before a witness and there would be no getting away with it."

April almost saw the thoughts flashing through Oscar's mind. He stepped back, lowering the pistol, and she breathed again. Her eyes flew to Lord Petteril's, but he wasn't looking at her. His eyes were locked with Oscar's, and in his hand he carried a small overnight bag.

"It's him," she said.

"I know," Petteril replied without releasing Oscar's eyes. "You saw her, didn't you? There was no need to kill him. It wasn't the end of the world."

A muscle twitched at the corner of Oscar's eye. "You...don't mind?" Oscar said cautiously.

"We all have human frailties, Oscar. But killing is something else."

Perplexed, Oscar stared back at him. Into the silence, came hurried footsteps, a woman's querulous voice. Oscar blinked and dropped his pistol back in his pocket. April wanted to run to Lord Petteril, but she seemed to be glued to the floor. It was Petteril who moved to stand by her as Mrs. Lindon and Miss Jones erupted into the room.

They stopped dead.

"What on earth are you all doing in my bedchamber?" Mrs. Lindon demanded. "Oscar?"

"I found the girl here, snooping. Petteril should dismiss her."

"Then he can do so in the privacy of his own house! Out, all of you."

"Actually," Lord Petteril said, unmoving, "I think you should send for your husband. April, perhaps you would..."

"There's no need," Miss Jones said sternly, glaring at April. "He's on his way, now we know the mistress never sent for me at all. Something havey-cavey's going on and *she's* at the root of it!"

"Actually, she isn't," Petteril said, turning to face the door as Mr. Lindon walked in, startled to see his wife's apartment full of people. "Oscar is."

"Oscar is what?" Lindon demanded. "What the devil is going on? Oscar? Petteril?"

Lord Petteril held up the bag. "I think if you show this to Hunter, he'll agree it belonged to Orr."

"What's that got to do with Oscar?" Even as he spoke the words, the dreadful suspicion began to darken his eyes.

"I found it in Oscar's room, sir."

An anguished sound issued from Mrs. Lindon's lips. They were white as she stared at her son. "You? *You?* Oh, Oscar..." She reached for him and he lashed out in fury, knocking her arm away.

"I *saw* you!" he burst out. It was almost a sob, "*You.* And..." He gasped, staring wildly around everyone in the room. Then he bolted, bumping his dazed father out of the way as he ran from the room.

He has a gun. April and Petteril started after him at the same time while Oscar's parents stared at each other in growing horror and fear.

Flying down the stairs, they were in time to see the front door close and dashed toward it. Petteril wrenched it open and April didn't even bother to close it behind them. They could see Oscar charging around the side of the house, as though fleeing for his life.

"He's going to the stables," April gasped, and sure enough, he ran past the edge of the formal garden where Laura and Lord Maxwell were standing together, staring after him.

"Oscar!" Laura called, pulling Hunter with her as she pursued her brother, not to the stables, but straight on to the wooded area behind the garden.

April and Petteril were faster, but not fast enough.

Just as they reached the first tree, they heard the deafening shot.

"Oh God," Petteril whispered, but he didn't slow down. He didn't even pause until they reached Oscar lying on the ground, the pistol still in his lifeless fingers.

Chapter Fourteen

The other guests had all gone home, even Dr. Rose. Piers, at Lindon's request, had stayed behind. Somehow, as though still in shock, Mr. and Mrs. Lindon had taken his advice, told their guests that Oscar had been taken ill—it accounted for their white, anxious faces—and explained the shot, overheard by some, as the gamekeeper after poachers in the wood.

"Probably the same ones who killed the man in my wood," Piers had added to one or two people. In face of Oscar's death and the pain of his family, the truth for truth's sake no longer mattered.

Dr. Rose knew, of course, but he had compassion enough not to even mention suicide. If all went well, the Lindons would at least avoid that shame and the burying of their beloved son in unhallowed ground. Now, he could rest in the church yard with the rest of his family.

"He couldn't live with what he had done," Lindon said, tears streaming unchecked down his cheeks. He sat on the sofa in the drawing room beside his wife, not touching. Laura sat close by, white as a sheet, staring straight ahead as though at nightmares on the backs of her eyelids. She had seen her brother's body.

Piers bowed his head in agreement. Privately, he thought that Oscar could not live with other people *knowing* what he had done and why, but there was no need to sully his father's honest grief.

"I—we... wanted to thank you," Lindon said. "I wish you hadn't found all this out. I wish it was like before. But since it can't be, I'm glad it was you." He looked up painfully. "Am I wrong to assume we can count on your continued discretion?"

"No," Piers said. "You are not wrong in that."

"What about that girl of yours?"

"April? Close-mouthed as they come."

Lindon nodded. He looked like an old man. "You will carry out Oscar's last wishes and look after my Laura?"

Laura's head jerked around to stare at him.

Piers said, "Of course I shall look out for her. But the looking *after* is down to her father or her husband."

"You don't want her because of the scandal," Mrs. Lindon said with contempt. "You know it is bound to be whispered about, even if just behind our backs. No one else will take her now."

"He never wanted me in the first place," Laura said irritably. "This is where all your machinations and Oscar's have led us. Well, no more. I shall not marry Lord Petteril or anyone else you come up with. I shall marry Lord Maxwell."

"Oh God." Lindon buried his face in his hands, while Laura frowned.

"What? He loves me. It isn't about my fortune, not anymore."

"No," her mother agreed harshly. "It is about the family of a suicide, tainted by scandal. It may be my fault but you are tainted with us. Lord Maxwell would not marry you now were your fortune three times the size it is. Even if he would, his family won't let him."

Laura's lips were white now. "Then it is all over," she whispered. "Everything is over..."

"No," Piers said forcefully. They all glanced at him in surprise, but it was Laura's gaze he held on to. "It is *never* over. Never even think it. There is always something, some hope, some new happiness around the corner. Trust me. I know. Hold on and it will come."

Tears started to Laura's eyes. "Why are you so kind to us?"

He tried to smile. "I suppose we have been friends a long time. I stand by that." Oscar had been his friend, had pulled him out of the river, shared games and laughter...

A gasp issued from Mrs. Lindon's mouth. She had grasped her husband's hand and held on to it so tightly that her fingers were white. And he didn't let go.

It was Laura who showed Piers to the door and threw her arms around his neck. "Thank you," she said and turned and ran upstairs as if all the fiends in hell were after her.

For a moment, Piers watched her, thinking not of her but of her brother, and let the misery of grief claim him.

LAURA DID NOT HESITATE. She went straight to Maxwell's bedchamber and knocked on his door. He opened it almost at once, still fully dressed, although he had thrown off his cravat. He stood back to let her in, then reached for her.

She eluded him, slipping past him to the window.

"They'll cover it up, but the whispers will be there. What Mama did. What Oscar did. Adultery, murder and suicide. None of it will be worse than Oscar lying there..."

"Laura." He started toward her, but again she warded him off.

"Don't," she uttered. "I understand. Just, please, go in the morning without saying goodbye. That is all I ask of you."

There was a moment's silence. Laura tried to make her legs work, to walk away from him, but it took a moment.

He said, "You promised to marry me."

"I release you," she said, and her laugh came out as a sob because it was what he had once said to her.

"I don't care about your family. I don't care about mine. I do not release you. Unless you don't love me."

She lifted her eyes to his in amazement. "I should say I don't. To save you from the awfulness that seems to be my family and my life. But I will not lie to you... *Maxwell!*" The last came out as a squeak as he swept her into his arms and kissed her fiercely. And then, in pain and gratitude, she cried like a baby on his shoulder.

APRIL HAD BEEN WAITING in the carriage for some time, shivering with apprehension. She was so relieved when he finally emerged from the house and climbed in to collapse on the seat opposite that she couldn't speak.

It might have been a blessing. Despite the darkness, she knew he was held together by a very slender thread. Once, he had almost taken the same way out as Oscar. A different method, different reasons, the same apparent impossibility of continuing to live.

She wished with all her being that Oscar had died by any other method than his own hand. The horses moved forward, taking the well worn road back to Haybury Court.

"They'll cover up the suicide," he said at last. "And everything else. It might work."

She nodded, still frightened to speak while fear swamped her. The silence stretched until he leaned forward and the carriage lamp light flickered over his gaunt, delicate face. She saw the pain and the tiredness—and the worry which seemed, bizarrely, to be directed at her.

"I'm sorry. I shouldn't have let you see the body."

"I seen worse," she snapped at once.

"Then what is it?"

"You!" she shouted, and to her horror tears started to her eyes. She dashed them angrily on the back of her sleeve. "Idiot! I don't want you *thinking* of Oscar, of *that*. What he done. I don't want..." She ran out of words and breath, but not, apparently, of tears, which she had to wipe this time on both sleeves.

The light flickered once more, but his eyes were steady on hers. He moved again, and she felt his hand close strongly over hers. She didn't even mind. Her fingers twisted, clinging to his.

"I won't, April," he said. "It was one moment, a moment I won't forget because of all I would have lost by it. You saved me, and I won't ever throw such a gift away."

She gazed at him, reading the truth and the strength she wanted to see there. At that moment, she believed it would always be true.

He sat back and she let him go reluctantly.

"Now," he said, "the mystery is solved. Tragedy doesn't mean we can't enjoy the countryside. I think you should learn to ride Maria's mare."

April sat up in instant delight. "Cor!"

A Sneak Peek: *Petteril's Ladybird* **(Lord Petteril Mysteries, Book 3)**

A pall of thick fog hung over London as Piers Withan, fifth Viscount Petteril, returned to his town house in May. Cold and damp as he undoubtedly was, he could not help comparing this arrival with his last, just over two months ago. Then, the house had been unoccupied, bare, and bleak, a symbol of grief and the unbearable life being forced upon him.

Now, he actually grinned as the girl beside him, April, leapt out of the curricle to get to the horses' heads moments before the footman ran out to take them. He could not cure her of the habit and wasn't sure he wanted to.

He alighted with marginally more grace, spared a pat for the near-horse's neck and strolled into his house.

"Welcome home, my lord," his impressive butler greeted him with what appeared to be a genuine smile.

Piers had employed him largely because his eyes occasionally twinkled. He could not abide Friday-faced butlers. "Thank you, Park. I trust everyone is well?"

"Indeed, sir. I hope your journey was not too trying?"

"Not until we reached London and the fog blinded us!"

"Sir Peter Haggard awaits you in the library, my lord," Park said, taking Piers's hat and coat and passing them to the waiting footman. "He said you were expecting him. Would you prefer to bathe and change before you receive him?"

"No, I'll do that afterward. Good day, Mrs. Park," he added cheerfully to the housekeeper who beamed at him.

"I'll send up tea and toast," she said.

Piers was surprised to find tea and toast was exactly what he wanted to scare the chill from his bones, so he grinned back at her and leapt upstairs, three at a time.

He was glad to find the library fire had been lit, though it was with more mixed feelings that he greeted his visitor who, in fact, was the one who had summoned him back to London from his country estate.

"Haggs," Piers said, holding out his hand, which Haggard strode over to shake.

"Withy!" His friend's harsh-featured face showed deep concern behind his grin. "Sorry to annoy you as soon as you're over the doorstep, but I thought you'd want to know. It looks bad for Austen."

"What happened?" Piers waved him to a chair. "Who the devil do they think he killed?"

"Barret Bootle."

"Er... Should I know the name?"

"No, he's several years older than us. Younger son of the Earl of Kinsley."

"Hence the danger. Why the devil do they think it was Percy Austen? Amiable fellow, Percy."

"Got a temper, though," Haggard said judiciously. "All the same, I'm sure he didn't do this. Trouble is, he quarrelled with Bootle the same day. You and I know if he was going to attack someone, he'd have done it then—or at least called Bootle out. Not gone home, brooded for several hours and then returned to shoot him in the back of the head."

Piers winced. "No. That doesn't sound like the Percy Austen I remember. What did they quarrel over?"

Haggard grimaced. "A woman. One Mrs. Eastleigh, a taking little widow whom Austen installed in a pleasant house in Kensington a few years ago. They parted ways last year and I believe Bootle took over the lease of both house and widow."

A footman brought in a heavy tray of tea things and a mountainous plate of toast. He smiled too, a welcome relief from the squalid little tale being told. His name was Francis and it was a pleasure as well as a small triumph to recognize his face.

"Go on," Piers said, when Francis had gone. He threw himself into the chair opposite his friend. "Where did the shooting happen?"

"In Mrs. Eastleigh's house," Haggs said grimly.

"Then isn't it more likely to have been Mrs. Eastleigh?"

"Her maid claims to have been with her when it happened. Besides…"

Piers felt a tightening in his stomach. This, he suspected, was the crux of the matter. "Besides what?" he asked with a sense of doom.

"The pistol he was shot with belonged to Austen. It was found next to the body and Austen admitted it was his."

Piers stared at him. "He left it there like a banner? A signature, acknowledging *I did this*?"

Haggard shrugged. "Stupid, I know. But the magistrate seems to think it suits a crime of such passion, even if he hasn't yet arrested him for it. Percy denies it, of course. And it's hardly the crime of a gentleman."

"Then why is he being pursued for it? Are the Bootles out for blood?"

"It would appear so."

Piers drank his tea and munched his way through a slice of toast and butter.

"What do you think we should do for him?" Haggard wondered. "Except try and find him a top-of-the-trees barrister."

Piers scowled. "We can't let it come to trial. He has a sister and an aunt and God knows how many dependents. Even if he got off, they'd all be ruined."

"I'm open to suggestion."

Piers put down his teacup and rose to pull the bell. "Send me Miss April," he said to the footman who appeared, and to Haggard, "She's good at stuff like this."

Haggard regarded him while he swallowed his last mouthful of toast. "Miss *April*," he repeated. "Surely you don't mean…?"

April herself breezed into the room like the sun breaking through a cloud. "Whatcher, sir?" she greeted Haggard with a grin. Even in an old-fashioned, unflattering dress, with a maid's cap crammed over her too-short golden locks, she was dazzling when she smiled.

"Good God," Haggard said.

Piers watched with some pride as recognition and then wonder filled his friend's ugly-attractive face.

"Oh dear," Haggard uttered.

"What d'you mean, *oh dear*?" April demanded. "I got jam on me face, or what?"

"Lord, no," Haggard said, recovering. "You look charmingly, I assure you."

April wrinkled her slightly upturned nose. "I know he told you, so there's no need to stare."

"Still as cheeky as Ape," Haggard remarked. "What on earth do the other servants say?"

"Nothing. They can't imagine it, especially 'cause I'm *Miss* April now, *his* assistant."

Piers interrupted. "We're going out in half an hour and you had better come with us. You'll have to wash and change."

She looked him up and down. "So will you."

"Indeed," he murmured as she all but skipped off. He kept his face bland and, he hoped, colour-free, as he faced Haggard once more.

Haggs said, "I congratulate you on the transformation. But you do know what people will say?"

Piers sighed. "Gossip dies from lack of oxygen. We've already been through it at Haybury Court."

"Maybe so, but you can't take her into Austen's aunt's drawing room with you!"

Piers considered. "All things are possible," he said vaguely. Then, seeing Haggard's expression, he added, "You know damned well I haven't touched her. And wouldn't."

"Won't stop other men trying."

"Well, they're liable to get more than they bargained for," Piers said with a twisted smile.

"Hmm." Haggard reached for another slice of toast. The mountain on the plate was severely reduced. "What is she, though? She's no stable lad anymore, and she doesn't behave like any maid I've ever come across. What the devil is an assistant?"

Piers considered. "One who assists. Like a secretary. Or a governess. Only she eats in the servants' hall, so I suppose she is an upper servant. Mrs. Park knows all about her."

"Do *you*?" Haggard asked, genuine anxiety in his eyes. After all, April had been living rough on the streets of St. Giles as a boy before Piers had employed her in his stable.

Piers was glad he had never told his friend that on their first encounter, April had been burgling his house. "I know enough," he said, making for the door. "I'll be twenty minutes."

*(READ THE REST IN **Petteril's Ladybird**, available late October 2023)*

About the Author

Mary Lancaster is a USA Today bestselling author of award winning historical romance and historical fiction. She lives in Scotland with her husband, one of three grown-up kids, and a small dog with a big personality.

Her first literary love was historical fiction, a genre which she relishes mixing up with romance and adventure in her own writing. Several of her novels feature actual historical characters as diverse as Hungarian revolutionaries, medieval English outlaws, and a family of eternally rebellious royal Scots. To say nothing of Vlad the Impaler.

More recently, she has enjoyed writing light, fun Regency romances, with occasional forays into the Victorian era. With its slight change of emphasis, *Petteril's Thief*, is her first Regency-set historical mystery.

CONNECT WITH MARY ON-line – she loves to hear from readers:

Email Mary: Mary@MaryLancaster.com

Website: http://www.MaryLancaster.com

Newsletter sign-up: https://marylancaster.com/newsletter/

Facebook: https://www.facebook.com/mary.lancaster.1656

Facebook Author Page: https://www.facebook.com/MaryLancasterNovelist/

Twitter: @MaryLancNovels https://twitter.com/MaryLancNovels

Bookbub: https://www.bookbub.com/profile/mary-lancaster